VINTAGE DREAMS

MAE ARCHER

MELBOURNE, AUSTRALIA

https://www.pishukinpress.com/

First Published 2023

Pishukin Press

Cover design: © Beaubelle | Dreamstime.com- Vintage Fashion Mannequins, Vector Set Photo, Created using Canva elements

Dyslexic Books edition: 9781922871497

Chapter 1

The pulsating rhythm of the music enveloped Allegra as she lost herself on the crowded dance floor of Hot Spot, her favorite weekend club. The clock on the wall was a mere formality; time was irrelevant in this kaleidoscope of lights and beats. The night had taken on a sultry, feverish quality, leaving a glistening sheen of sweat on her skin. Allegra's body moved with a hypnotic grace, her flared nautical pants swaying to the intoxicating melody.

But a peculiar sensation tingled down her spine amidst the flashing lights and undulating bodies. She was being watched. Her instincts were sharp, and without a second thought, she subtly turned her head, her raven hair cascading like a waterfall, to seek the source of her unease. And there he was, on the balcony overhead.

Her mysterious night watcher. She'd been aware of his presence for weeks, a lone figure in a sea of revelers, dressed in a suit and tie that marked him as a stark contrast to the casual crowd. He never danced or flirted with the women who approached him. Instead, he remained detached, his gaze locked on her.

Allegra had wondered when he would make a move, approach her with a few well-practiced lines. But he hadn't. The possibility of him being a stalker had crossed her mind during the second week, leading her to take precautions when leaving the club. Yet, as far as she could tell, he always left well before her, as if he were searching for the courage to approach her, and, when he couldn't find it, retreated into the night.

Tonight, however, was different. Tonight, they would finally speak. She continued dancing, her movements slowing into languorous, seductive motions, her every move an invitation. She seized the moment when she saw him retreat from the balcony, heading for the bar. With a nod from the bartender, she slipped through the service entrance, quickly rounding the corner to stand at the mouth of the alley.

She watched as Night Watcher exited the club. Hot Spot was nestled in the heart of downtown, its bright neon lights casting an eerie glow on the bustling sidewalks. Witnesses abounded, and Allegra knew that this risky confrontation needed an audience.

Silent as a shadow, she fell in step behind him, her strides lengthening until she was walking beside him in the well-lit street. She wasted no time. 'I thought tonight would be the night you asked me for my number.'

He jerked to a halt, his brown hair falling over his forehead to frame his boyish face. Surprise flashed in his wide eyes as he struggled to respond. 'Why would you think that?' His voice trembled with un-certainty.

His recovery impressed Allegra. He'd appeared on the verge of choking just moments ago. 'It's usually what a man does after he's checked out the merchandise. And you, my friend, have been checking me out for a few weeks.' She tilted her head, her hands resting confidently on her hips. Her outfit, a vintage 1960s ensemble of nautical pants, silver platform shoes, and a black crisscross brassiere top, was attention-grabbing, yet it was just an everyday part of her wardrobe. She'd been a devotee of vintage fashion since her teenage years.

His gaze dropped briefly to her cleavage be-fore snapping back to her face, his Adam's ap-ple bobbing as he swallowed hard. He ran a hand through his hair and glanced over her shoulder. 'What makes you so sure I was checking you out?'

'I know these things,' Allegra replied with self-as-suredness. Confidence had always been her con-stant companion. Framed by thick lashes, her blue eyes mirrored her mother's, and her raven hair cas-caded into loose curls down her back. She'd drawn admiring glances from the opposite sex since her breasts had first filled out her school dress at thirteen.

'And I know you're a lawyer,' she added.

His eyes narrowed in suspicion. 'How do you know that?'

'That suit is a dead giveaway.' His Armani suit, the latest season's dove gray pure wool and silk, hugged his athletic frame with a slim-fit jacket. 'Corporate law?' she ventured.

He nodded.

'Allegra.' She extended her hand, feeling a tingling sensation as their skin met.

'Emmett.'

This unexpected attraction surprised her. She hadn't expected to feel drawn to her Night Watcher. Initially, she had intended to shake his cage, to confront him and dismiss him from her thoughts. Yet, there was something about him, something that piqued her curiosity.

'You don't strike me as the Hot Spot type,' Allegra remarked, breaking the silence. Hot Spot was renowned for playing the latest tracks, catering to the younger crowd. 'I would have pegged you as more of a High Lounge guy.'

'I went to High Lounge with my colleagues a few weeks ago,' Emmett explained. 'It wasn't to my taste. I hoped Hot Spot would be a better fit.'

'And is it?' Allegra halted and turned to face him, her gaze probing.

'I'm still deciding.' Emmett maintained unbroken eye contact.

Allegra's breath quickened as they reached her destination. 'This is my stop.' She gestured toward Marcy's Place, a small diner that had become her post-club ritual.

Emmett seemed on the verge of saying something but hesitated, biting his lip instead. 'It was nice meeting you,' he finally offered.

She sensed his unspoken desire to join her but his hesitancy to ask. He didn't fit her usual mold; she favored confident, flirtatious men. Emmett was different, intriguing. 'Would you like to join me?' she impulsively asked.

He nodded, a smile tugging at his lips. Holding the door open, he waited for her to pass before following her inside.

Seated at their booth, Emmett's gaze roamed the eclectic clientele of Marcy's Place. Most were women from the nearby strip joint, their alluring attire hinting at their profession, yet the atmosphere was welcoming.

'You're early, girlfriend,' Joleen, a statuesque African-American drag queen, greeted Allegra upon her arrival.

Emmett's gaze flitted to Joleen and quickly averted. Joleen stood tall at six-foot-four, donned in jeans and platform shoes, her Adam's apple a vestige of her true identity. 'Well, hello, honey,' Joleen purred, eying Emmett appreciatively. 'You're a sight for sore eyes.'

As she leaned over, Joleen's chicken fillet—padding used to enhance her bust—fell out. 'Damn it, that's been happening all night,' she complained, hastily readjusting it.

'You bought too small a bra,' Allegra pointed out as she stood up, her nimble fingers loosening Joleen's bra straps at the back. 'Your cup size is correct, but you need a wider back.' She pointed to the flimsy straps. 'You're a strapping girl and need proper support.'

'But I enjoy wearing pretty colors,' Joleen pouted, gazing down at her enhanced assets. 'Don't they make my girls look pretty?' She glanced at Emmett.

He blushed and stammered, 'Yes, very pretty.'

Joleen beamed. 'Well, you've got a proper gentleman here.'

Allegra couldn't help but chuckle. 'You can still have pretty bras and get support; you just have to shop at the right place.'

'And you're going to take me to these right shops?' Joleen raised an eyebrow.

'Okay, fine, we'll go bra shopping,' Allegra agreed.

'Pick you up at 12,' Joleen insisted.

'Make it 1. I need some extra sleep.'

Joleen shook her head. 'You're acting like a grandma. Live while you're alive; sleep while you're dead.'

Allegra shot her a playful scowl. 'Well, maybe Grandma shouldn't take you shopping if you're going to end up in a granny bra.'

'I'm just teasing.' Joleen affectionately caressed Allegra's face. 'You know you're my beautiful.'

Allegra sniffled, her emotions touched by Joleen's words. 'I'll have my usual.'

Joleen turned her attention to Emmett. 'What would you like to eat, sugar?'

Emmett glanced at the menu, appearing somewhat bewildered. 'I'll have what she's having.'

'Okay, two Trucker Breakfasts coming right up,' Joleen announced with a smile.

Allegra tapped her nails on the table, her thoughts momentarily drifting to her recent journey through breast cancer and remission. She'd only received the all-clear three months ago, and while she was grateful for the chance to grow older, something had changed within her during her battle with the disease. It was as if her brain had not yet processed that the danger was over and that she could now embrace life rather than just survive.

'That's a hearty breakfast,' Emmett remarked, drawing her attention back.

Allegra smiled. 'I'm not worried about calories; I'll dance them off tomorrow.'

'Is clubbing a nightly routine for you?'

She sipped her hot chocolate and shook her head. 'I take dance classes.'

'Really?'

'Tomorrow is ballroom,' she continued.

'Are you a professional dancer?'

Allegra met Emmett's curious gaze. 'You've seen me on the dance floor, haven't you? No, this is just the only exercise I can stand.'

Emmett's inquisitive look persisted, but Allegra chose not to reveal the deeper reasons behind her love for dancing. The chemotherapy and radiation treatment had led to weight gain, and she detested how it made her feel. Running, the gym, and even yoga had failed to captivate her. Dancing was her sanctuary; it allowed her to lose herself in the rhythm and silence the inner noise.

After a pause, she confessed, 'I hate the thought of traditional exercise. Dancing helps me stay active without feeling like I'm working out.'

Joleen returned with their plates, laden with hearty food. Allegra dug in, her hunger cramps giving way to contentment. Emmett, however, ate slowly, clearly unaccustomed to such a heavy meal late at night.

'Is this not your type of food?' Allegra asked, a hint of concern in her voice.

'No, it's good,' Emmett assured her. 'I'm just not used to such a heavy meal at this hour.'

Allegra shrugged, savoring the sensation of indulgence after a night of dancing. 'I love feeling this way after a night out—full and blissfully tired. It's my way of ending the night.'

She dropped her fork on the ground, stood to pick it up, and walked to the counter for a replacement.

'And how do you find your date?' Jolene asked, already waiting for her, holding a fork.

'Flirtation only.' She'd thought she'd confront her Night Stalker and be done with his annoying attention. Instead, she'd found Emmett's charm surprising. Still, he wasn't her type, and he wasn't worth pursuing any further. He was strictly dating and commitment, and Allegra was only interested in flirting and fun. However, there was no harm in enjoying some harmless flirtation before she cut him loose.

'Shame.' Jolene smiled at Emmett. 'He's a good change of pace for you.'

Allegra frowned.

'You know—men can be cute and smart at the same time.'

This was a speech Joleen had been making for the past few months, taking snipes at Allegra's dating choices. Allegra snatched the fork and returned to Emmett, noticing the way his eyes lingered on her hips. She added more pep to her walk, enjoying the flushing of his cheeks when she caught him.

She slid into the seat opposite and resumed eating. 'So, were you ever going to talk to me, or do you enjoy stalking?' Allegra asked, her voice laced with a mix of amusement and suspicion.

She enjoyed watching the flush creeping across his face, feeling a tingle of delight at his discomfort.

'I wasn't sure I was your type,' he admitted, his voice revealing a hint of uncertainty.

'I don't have a type,' Allegra countered, holding her cup between her hands as she scowled at him over the edge.

'Either you're being coy, or you're in denial,' Emmett replied, a touch of disbelief in his voice.

'I beg your pardon?' Allegra's surprise was clear. Most men would have backed by now, fearing they were offending her but not Emmet.

'So it is denial,' Emmett said, nonchalantly adding maple syrup to his buttermilk pancakes. 'You might not consciously realize it, but you have a type. You go for young men with big muscles, toothy smiles, and flirtatious ways. It suggests you like your men malleable.'

'I do not!' Allegra protested, remembering Joleen's advice, and felt a flush on color her cheeks. She shifted in her seat, feeling uncomfortable at this power dynamics change.

Emmett quirked an eyebrow and waited. Damnit, he knew he'd gotten to her. She didn't like that he could read her.

'Okay, so maybe I have a type,' Allegra admitted after a brief pause. 'But that doesn't mean I wouldn't have given you a chance.'

'Would you have said yes if I'd asked you out?' Emmett asked, doubt in his voice.

'Yes,' Allegra responded, wanting to rattle him. He stared her down, and she knew he wasn't buying it. She hesitated and added, 'Maybe.'

Emmett lifted his coffee cup in a toast, amused by her honesty. 'You're surprisingly forthright. I would blame it on alcohol, but I don't think you drink.'

'I don't,' Allegra confirmed with a shrug. 'And I am honest. I don't see the point in artifice. And the truth is I probably wouldn't have said yes if you had approached me in the club, but I am most definitely intrigued now.'

She gazed into his eyes, seeing him sizing her up. He was right; he wasn't her usual choice. She wanted men she could enjoy the pleasures of the flesh with no emotional entanglements. Emmett was not the safe choice for her. He wasn't easily manipulated and didn't shy away from heavy emotions. She heard Joleen's refrain from earlier, 'men can be cute and smart at the same time.' Maybe it was time she found out.

Emmett straightened his shoulders. 'So, I'll pick you up at 8 pm tomorrow.'

Allegra's response was a smile. 'All right.' A flutter of butterflies danced in her stomach. She was definitely taking a risk, but Emmett intrigued her.

They exchanged phone numbers, and as they finished their meal, Emmett made his way to the cashier, intent on paying. Allegra, however, waved him away with a casual gesture. 'This isn't our date,' she explained.

'Let's call this our pre-date meet-up. My car is out back, and I'll give you a lift home.'

'I usually just catch a taxi.'

'I insist. After all, I need to know where to pick you up.'

Allegra nodded. 'I'll be a moment.' She walked to Jolene. 'Emmett is giving me a lift.' Joleen nodded, understanding her code. A woman couldn't be too careful these days getting into a car with a stranger. Allegra would take a photo of his license plates and send them to Joleen before getting into the car.

He walked her to his car, and Allegra provided directions. Ten minutes later, they arrived at a winding driveway that led to a magnificent Queen Anne mansion. As Emmett turned off the car's engine, she saw his awed expression. 'Do you live here all by yourself?' he asked, his gaze fixed on the grand mansion with its rounded turrets that loomed eerily in the darkness.

'Yes,' Allegra replied as she retrieved her keys. 'I just moved in.'

'Oh,' Emmett responded.

She knew he was thinking she didn't seem like the typical heiress to such a place. This was old money. 'I inherited it,' Allegra added.

'So, I'll pick you up from here tomorrow,' Emmett said, hesitating momentarily.

She knew he was deciding whether or not to kiss her. Usually, she leaned into the first kiss, wanting to get to the good part and let passion sweep her away, but she suddenly felt shy. She wanted to go on a proper date with Emmett and get to know him rather than doing her usual sleep and dump.

Unlocking her front door, Allegra leaned over and kissed his cheek, breathing in his cologne, fighting the urge to nuzzle into his neck and hold him tight as he held himself still. 'I'll see you tomorrow,' she said before stepping inside her house. She leaned against the door and listened to his car driving away, her pulse fluttering. That was unexpected.

She walked up the stairs, hearing a creak from the floor above her as if someone was creeping about, and paused, her hand clenched on the banister, her eyes peering up as she listened intently. There was no further sound. A yawn surprised her, and a wave of fatigue swept over her. She needed sleep. She finished climbing the stairs, quickly wiped off her makeup, and changed into a dusty pink satin cami nightdress before slipping in the satin nightsheets of the four-poster bed, sinking into slumber.

Allegra awoke with a start, her senses jolting to life. The room enveloped her in an unfamiliar embrace, and for a fleeting moment, she struggled to place herself. It was a sensation not entirely foreign to her, having stirred from slumber in many an unfamiliar bed next to enigmatic men after nights of reckless revelry. Yet, this time, the throbbing ache of a customary hangover was conspicuously absent.

As the minutes ticked by, the veil of slumber lifted, and the room's interior emerged from the shadows. Moonlight filtered through the heavy damask curtains, revealing a stately four-poster bed, commanding attention beneath the intricately molded ceiling. Allegra's consciousness whispered that she was in Henry's house, a mansion with a storied past, now that it was her own.

She pushed herself upright, pushing away the cascade of ebony locks from her face. Sleep would not reclaim her, not now. A faint creaking sound pricked at her senses, the eerie echo of footsteps traversing ancient wooden floors. Goosebumps prickled her skin as unease settled in. Could the tales of this mansion's spectral inhabitants hold some truth? Henry had brushed aside such rumors, having lived here for decades, but Allegra was no stranger to the power of an old house's haunted history.

Her nightclothes clung to her frame, a flimsy shield against the spectral possibilities. Courage found her, though, as she knew she could not cower in the face of ghostly illusions. Turning on the light, she ventured into the hallway, casting a curious gaze down the curved staircase, a portal to the shadows below. Silence greeted her, a chilling void.

'Is someone there?' she called hesitantly, feeling the theatricality of her vulnerability. Yet, there was no response, no sinister figure cloaked in darkness wielding a phantom blade.

'Enough of this, Allegra,' she chided herself, the resolute tone in her voice echoing in the empty corridors. 'Ghosts do not exist.'

Turning back to her room, she tugged on her sturdy boots resolved to investigate the empty bedrooms down the hall. The clatter of her heels echoed through the house, a haunting cadence that tugged at her nerves, but she pressed on.

Approaching the door to the first guest room, a sense of trepidation enveloped her. Doubt encroached upon her resolve, and she retraced her steps, descending the stairs with her cell phone in hand.

'Jolene, it's Allegra,' she said when her friend answered, a hint of drowsiness in Jolene's voice.

'I thought we were hitting the shops at 1,' Jolene murmured, her voice tinged with sleepiness.

'It's a woman's prerogative to change her mind,' Allegra replied with a forced lightness, omitting her real motive for fleeing the house.

Draping herself in a coat, she snatched her handbag from the foyer, locking the front door behind her. Each step toward the garage bore the weight of unseen eyes upon her, a disconcerting sensation that she dared not acknowledge. She swung open the door to the vintage 1957 Cadillac, 'Ruby,' as Henry had affectionately named it, and peeled away, leaving behind the oppressive atmosphere of the mansion.

Arriving at Jolene's haven, she found her friend donned in a pink housecoat, her head freshly bald from the absence of a wig. 'I need coffee before we can leave,' Jolene declared.

Allegra nodded, seeking refuge in the mundane as they settled in for coffee and conversation. 'So, what happened with the cutie pie last night?' Jolene inquired, her eyes sparkling with curiosity.

'Nothing much. We're going on a date tonight?' Allegra said, casually sweeping up her using the stainless steel toaster to see her reflection.

'Really.' Jolene quirked an eyebrow as she drank coffee.

'I don't see it leading anywhere. He's too... safe.' Allegra said. 'The only reason I said yes is because of you.'

'Then I'm doing something right,' Joleen laughed wickedly and returned to her bedroom to get ready.

Chapter 2

Emmett Dennison sat at a corner table in Marcy's Place, his eyes never straying far from Allegra as she savored her meal. He'd been watching her for several weeks, each night making a silent promise to himself that he would approach her, but the courage had continually eluded him. The first time he had seen her had been a revelation, a stark contrast to his own life.

Envy had swept over him as he observed her carefree demeanor. She arrived on the dance floor before anyone else, moving with a joy and abandon that fascinated him. It was a feeling he couldn't recall ever experiencing. Even in childhood, his destiny had been decided before he knew himself.

It wasn't just her stunning beauty, with her azure eyes and dark, flowing hair, that captivated him. It was her attitude, the way she moved through life as if every moment were an adventure waiting to happen. He remembered the night an unwelcome suitor had approached her on the dance floor, only to have her respond with absurdly exaggerated aerobics moves, sending the bewildered man scuttling away in embarrassed confusion. That night, Emmett had laughed spontaneously, a sound that had long been absent from his life.

But when Allegra confronted him outside the club, everything changed. Her sudden presence had thrown him off balance, leaving him at a loss for words. He was accustomed to being in control in his world, but she had disrupted his carefully orchestrated plans.

Now, as she delicately bit her pancake, she eyed him curiously while he fought to keep his gaze off her lush lips.

'So, were you ever going to talk to me, or do you enjoy stalking?' Allegra had asked, her voice laced with a mix of amusement and suspicion.

Emmett felt a flush creeping across his face. This wasn't how he had envisioned their first encounter. 'I wasn't sure I was your type,' he admitted, his voice revealing a hint of uncertainty.

He had witnessed her flirting and dancing with young, muscular men on previous nights, and it had dissuaded him from approaching her. 'I don't have a type,' Allegra countered.

'Either you're being coy, or you're in denial,' Emmett replied, a touch of disbelief in his voice. He had a knack for spotting lies, but she thoroughly disarmed him in this instance. She was watching him with innocent eyes. Did she really not know?

'I beg your pardon?' Allegra's surprise was clear.

'So it is denial,' Emmett said, nonchalantly adding maple syrup to his buttermilk pancakes. 'You might not consciously realize it, but you do have a type. You go for young men with big muscles, toothy smiles, and flirtatious ways. It suggests you like your men malleable.'

'I do not!' Allegra protested.

Emmett detected a flicker of doubt in her voice and couldn't help but feel a sense of satisfaction. He had successfully rattled her cage, turning the tables from his earlier awkwardness.

'Okay, so maybe I do have a type,' Allegra admitted after a brief pause. 'But that doesn't mean I wouldn't have given you a chance.'

He gripped his fork harder. He hadn't expected her to admit it. The woman he had expected to meet was one of manipulation and guile. 'Would you have said yes if I'd asked you out?' Emmett inquired, his interest piqued.

'Yes,' Allegra responded, then hesitated. 'Maybe.'

Emmett quirked an eyebrow, amused by her honesty. 'You're surprisingly forthright. I would blame it on alcohol, but I don't think you drink.' In all the time he had watched her, he'd never seen her drink anything other than a water bottle, even as different men approached her with various alcoholic concoctions to try and entice her away from the dance floor.

'I don't,' Allegra confirmed with a shrug. 'And I am honest. I don't see the point in artifice. And the truth is that I probably wouldn't have said yes if you had approached me in the club, but I am most definitely intrigued now.'

Her eyes bore into him, a mixture of curiosity and allure he was unaccustomed to. Usually, women regarded him as a safe choice—a man with good prospects, a dependable provider. But Allegra was unaware of his career or status, and he knew from watching her that these qualities held no sway over her criteria. Straightening his shoulders, he no longer felt timid or out of place. 'So, I'll pick you up at 8 pm tomorrow night.'

Allegra's response was a smile. 'All right.'

He had to fight to keep the surprise showing on his face. He really must have made an impression.

They exchanged phone numbers, and as they finished their meal, Emmett made his way to the cashier, intent on paying. Allegra, however, waved him away with a casual gesture. 'This isn't our date,' she explained.

'Let's call this our pre-date meet-up. My car is out back, and I'll give you a lift home.'

'I usually just catch a taxi.'

Emmett insisted. 'I insist. After all, I need to know where to pick you up.'

Allegra spoke briefly to Jolene before joining him. He walked her to his car, and Allegra provided directions. Ten minutes later, they arrived at a winding driveway that led to a magnificent Queen Anne mansion. As Emmett turned off the car's engine, he couldn't help but be awed by the sight. 'Do you live here all by yourself?' he asked, his gaze fixed on the grand mansion with its rounded turrets that loomed eerily in the darkness.

'Yes,' Allegra replied as she retrieved her keys. 'I just moved in.'

'Oh,' Emmett responded, his curiosity piqued. She didn't seem like the typical heiress to such a place.

'I inherited it,' Allegra added.

He didn't think she would admit the truth. 'So, I'll pick you up from here tomorrow,' Emmett said, hesitating momentarily. Should he kiss her, or would that be presumptuous?

Unlocking her front door, Allegra leaned over and planted a kiss on his cheek. 'I'll see you tomorrow,' she said before stepping inside her house.

As Emmett walked back to his car, he couldn't help but whistle. He picked up his phone and found Virgina's phone number. 'Made contact,' he typed and hit send. He took one last look at the mansion and drove back down the winding driveway. He couldn't believe his luck in achieving his goal.

Virginia called as he parked in the underground garage of his apartment. 'You've spoken to her?' she demanded, her voice high-pitched yet hushed so her husband wouldn't hear.

'Yes.'

Virginia breathed out a sigh of relief. 'And she's exactly like I told you. A conniving gold-digger?' Virginia Summer was the niece of the late Henry Mansfield, whose will had left the mansion to a certain Allegra Kenton.

Emmett hesitated, replaying his conversation with Allegra. She had been surprisingly forthright, admitting any slight artifice, but it wouldn't do him any good to say that to Virginia. At least in his mind, Emmett's task was simple: get the will overturned so Virginia could rezone the land.

'So how do we proceed? Do we put in the paperwork?' Virginia demanded.

He could see her in his mind's eye, chewing her thumb cuticle nervously. They'd been friends since college when they worked on the law journal together. Virginia Summer had been living a lie, leading her husband to believe she owned the entire property, and now she was in a time crunch. Her husband, Tim Summer, owner of Summer Construction, had already invested thousands of dollars in drawing up plans and seeking investors for his next development: the sprawling mansion that had stood untouched for years was his golden ticket. It was an eyesore to the city's developers, a prime piece of real estate waiting to be transformed into a lucrative commercial zone. Virginia needed the will overturned yesterday so she could salvage her marriage and wealth.

'First, we need to get leverage.' He remembered Allegra's statement that she'd inherited the mansion, a truth disguised as a lie. Virginia had told him the deceit she had practiced in tricking her vulnerable uncle, Henry, into writing her into his will. If there was one thing he hated, it was con artists who used their beauty and charm to wreak havoc and destruction on vulnerable people. This time, Allegra would meet her match, and he would take pleasure in making her pay for her lies.

Emmett didn't immediately turn on the lights when he returned home after the exhilarating date with Allegra. He savored the quiet solitude that enveloped him, a rare luxury in his life. Typically, he didn't stay up late, and fatigue descended as he settled into his favorite chair. But he craved a few moments to reflect on the extraordinary evening he'd just experienced.

He'd spent nights watching Allegra, trying to work up the courage to put his plan into motion, yet never feeling the time was right. Then, last night, she'd surprised him by letting him know she knew he was watching her when he thought he was spying on her in the safety of darkness. She wasn't quite what she had expected, but that didn't matter. Virginia needed his help, but more importantly, this was a chance to get some excitement into his mundane life. He was thrust into playing a spy to collect information on Allegra to fight the will. After tonight's date, he would return to his regular mundane life, and the beautiful Allegra would once more return to her nights of frivolity and dancing. He sighed, remembering her beautiful smile.

Suddenly, a blinding light burst into his eyes, making him wince and shield his face with his hand. His brother Rhys was standing next to the window, the curtains wrenched back, the morning sunlight pouring in.

'Why are you on the couch? You shouldn't sleep on the couch. You sleep on the bed,' Rhys chided.

Emmett groaned as he sat up. 'I was going to get to bed but fell asleep here.' He rubbed his sore neck, feeling the stiffness from his awkward nap. Rhys had spent the night at Betty's, their former housekeeper turned babysitter, to give Emmett a much-needed evening to himself. She greeted Emmett, and he walked her to the door after he paid her.

'But a couch isn't for sleeping,' Rhys insisted after Emmett had walked Betty out.

Emmett sighed and got up, heading to the kitchen. He retrieved a carton of orange juice from the fridge, ready to drink from it directly, but Rhys's horrified gasp stopped him in his tracks.

'Alright, alright,' Emmett conceded, grabbing a glass and pouring himself some juice. 'Theoretically, you can also sleep on a couch. In some cultures, it's quite common. They have to optimize space.'

'Really?' Rhys asked, his curiosity piqued.

Emmett nodded as he sipped his juice. 'Absolutely. People all over the world make the most of their living spaces.'

Rhys continued to question Emmett, who was relieved when his brother's attention eventually shifted to his computer. Rhys had a habit of researching various topics, hopefully keeping him occupied long enough for Emmett to steal a shower.

As the warm water flowed over him, Emmett couldn't help but sing, feeling an unusual sense of contentment. However, his moment of serenity was disrupted when he stepped out of the shower and found Rhys waiting in the bathroom.

'You're singing,' Rhys observed, his tone puzzled.

Emmett, toweling himself dry, replied, 'Some people like to sing in the shower. The acoustics are fantastic. In fact, some musicians even record their music in bathrooms.'

'Really,' Rhys said, appearing unconvinced. 'Wait. You're avoiding answering my question.' Rhys put his hand on his ear and tugged. 'I asked you why you slept on the couch, and you didn't answer. And now I asked you why you were singing, and you didn't want to tell me either. Something unusual has happened.'

Emmett walked to the closet and began dressing. He noticed Rhys's persistent frown and realized that distraction wouldn't work this time. While Rhys wasn't very perceptive in reading emotional cues, he was excellent at noticing changes in routine as these unsettled him. While Emmett knew Rhys's adherence to routine was a symptom of him being on the spectrum, he was also feeling weary that his life was becoming smaller as he accommodated his brother's needs.

'Alright, Rhys,' Emmett began. 'Something unusual happened last night. I met a woman, and we're going on a date tonight.' He'd wanted to avoid telling him anything about Allegra, as his date was an unusual occurrence, but Rhys would not be fobbed off with vague excuses. He needed blunt honesty and clear communication.

'But tonight is the rubric championship,' Rhys protested.

'Yes, but I also said that I might have to work, and so would have to reschedule,' Emmett reminded him.

'But you're not working. You are going out on a date.'

'Yes, I am,' Emmett said. 'So Betty can take you instead,' Emmett explained, referring to their babysitter. 'And then we could have a special night tomorrow, just us.'

'But you said you'd take me,' Rhys insisted.

'I did, but sometimes plans change,' Emmett replied evenly. 'You'll still have today to do whatever you want together.' He realized he had been accommodating Rhys's needs for too long and neglected his own. It was time to change. He had to use this as an opportunity to prepare Rhys for his future. After this covert operation with Allegra was over, it was time for Emmett to get out into the dating world again.

Rhys eventually accepted Emmett's compromise, and they spent the day together, playing video games and enjoying each other's company. As the clock ticked away, Emmett felt the impending date looming closer. Even though he knew this wasn't a real date, at least for him, he still felt blood thrumming through his veins in excitement at seeing Allegra. 'Down boy,' he chastised himself. 'This was a one-time thing.'

He had to use this date as his one opportunity to get information from Allegra about Henry. After tonight, he would vanish back into obscurity, and Allegra would return to her life as the Dancing Queen of Hot Spot.

At 6:30 p.m., Emmett began preparing for his date with Allegra. He showered, donned his best slacks and shirt, and carefully slicked back his hair. But looking at himself in the mirror, he felt like he resembled a lawyer rather than the mysterious man he wanted to be.

'Damn,' he muttered, yanking off his tie and discarding his shirt. After rummaging through his wardrobe, he found a white t-shirt and a stylish blue blazer that felt more like him. After all, he had gotten this far by getting Allegra to date against her usual type. He now needed to prick her curiosity enough to tell him about herself, give him something Virginia could use to overturn the will.

Emmett then drove Rhys to Betty's, promising he'd be back by 11 p.m.

'Have a great night,' Betty wished him, and Rhys, although silent, nodded in acknowledgment.

Emmett walked out of the house with a swagger. He couldn't wait to see Allegra.

Chapter 3

After a day of bra shopping and lunch with Jolene, Allegra returned home, brimming with anticipation. As she drove up her driveway, the grandeur of the house beckoned to her, its potential hidden beneath weathered facades, peeling paint, and leaning fence posts. Her vintage fashion inclinations thrived on uncovering hidden gems, transforming the discarded into something beautiful.

Stepping inside, she couldn't help but chastise herself for entertaining the notion of ghosts in this place. The house seemed to embrace her, recognizing her kindred spirit, an unspoken promise of shared dreams.

Her steps led her to the kitchen, where leftover pizza beckoned her. But her excitement gave way to unease when she discovered only two slices instead of the three she remembered. Her skin prickled as clarity dawned—not ghosts, but squatters. Hastily, she donned her attire, resolved to confront the intruders.

Leaving the house, she felt unseen eyes once more, a chilling sensation that she fiercely resisted. She reached her 1957 Cadillac, parked with a flourish, and sped away, putting distance between herself and the mansion.

Parking by a blind spot beneath a curve of nature strip, she climbed a nearby tree, dropping over the two-meter-high fence as she resolved to eliminate the sentimental tree that had compromised her safety. Her heart raced as she approached her back door, crouched behind hedges and hidden from view. Through the kitchen window, she spied the intruder, their feet protruding from beneath the fridge.

With a taser clutched in hand, she burst through the backdoor, her surprise sending the pizza crashing to the floor. But her assailant was no ghost or sinister specter—it was a child. A shock of recognition coursed through her as she met the child's blue eyes.

'Who are you?' Allegra stammered, her voice trembling.

The girl's response struck like a lightning bolt. 'I'm your daughter.'

Goosebumps danced along Allegra's arms. She recognized herself in the child, a reflection of her own past. 'What?' she demanded, struggling to process the revelation.

'Thirteen years ago, you gave me up for adoption,' the girl explained, handing her a document.

Allegra took it and read. For a moment, the words blurred as emotions coursed through her. She took a deep breath and saw that she was looking at her gynecology report. She flashed back to lying on an exam table, staring at the ceiling as her womb was invaded. Just before she sank under anesthetic, she knew she had made the wrong decision. Allegra should never have signed that piece of paper, but it was too late. She had made a promise and had to see it through, or she would break Amy's heart. Amy, who had so desperately wanted a baby for ten years and ravaged her body to achieve her dream.

In turmoil, she averted her gaze, leaning heavily on the kitchen counter. 'Mom,' the girl reached out, pulling at her hand.

'I'm not your mother,' Allegra snapped, recoiling from the touch, wrestling with the demons of her past.

A torrent of emotions swirled within her as she realized the gravity of the situation. She had never wanted children, fearing she would perpetuate the cycle of pain from her own upbringing. She had relinquished that responsibility to someone more capable – Amy.

'I mean, Amy is your mother,' Allegra correct-ed herself, forcing a smile. 'Why don't we call her to come and get you?' Allegra forced a smile.

The girl blinked away tears. 'Don't you know?'

'Know what?' Allegra said as she searched for her phone.

'My mom died. My dad, too.'

Allegra looked up in shock. 'What?'

She couldn't believe it. She felt a stab of pain. Amy was one of the most beautiful people she had known. She was made to be a mother, and while it had cost Allegra to help her, she had walked away and never looked back because she knew Amy would love the baby in a way she never would.

'They were killed by a drunk driver six months ago,' the girl said.

'I'm so sorry, Amethyst,' Allegra said. She should have known, but she and Amy had drift-ed apart. Allegra knew Amy didn't want any reminders that the baby wasn't hers, while Alle-gra didn't want to be confronted with her deci-sion. There had probably been a write-up in the newspaper, but while she had been fighting her cancer battle, her life had shrunk to the hospital cubicle where she received her chemotherapy, the bathroom where she vomited semi-regularly post-chemo, and the bed where she fell into death-like sleep in-between.

'You know my name,' Amethyst said.

'I gave you that name,' Allegra said. It was what she had named all her dolls when she was small, and Amy had promised that if the baby was a girl, that's what her name would be. Allegra had been ambivalent. She wasn't sure whether she wanted her past to be bound up in the new life she had helped create, but in the end, the choice hadn't been hers.

Amethyst smiled, and Allegra felt a twisting inside of her. It was like looking in a mirror.

'I knew it. I knew it was you when I saw you the first time.'

'The first time...' Allegra asked, still reeling from hearing about Amy passing.

'When I found your medical records, I googled and tracked you down. I saw you at the Prime Awards and then followed you home.'

The Prime Awards was an amateur dancing competition, and it was the first time she had competed with her dance partner, Mark.

The girl's eyes shimmered with adoration. 'You looked so beautiful dancing in that blue dress. I want to be just like you.'

Allegra felt the burden of her past decisions weighing heavily. She needed to get the girl out of the house and break the truth about her conception gently.

'We have to call home. We have to call your family,' Allegra said, reaching for her phone.

'Please don't,' the girl pleaded, her eyes filled with fear. 'Please don't let her take me.'

Allegra's heart constricted at the desperation in the girl's voice. 'Who?' she asked, trying to understand.

Before she could receive an answer, the doorbell rang, and a woman's voice called out from outside. The girl panicked, disappearing through the backdoor, leaving Allegra torn between following her and answering the door.

'Ms. Kenton, it's Officer Sanders. Please open up,' the voice demanded.

Allegra hurried toward the front door, the girl's unexplained disappearance haunting her thoughts.

Allegra was relieved to have an excuse to pause her conversation with Amethyst. She had to tell Amethyst the truth, but first, she had to get her into a safe environment. Amethyst had lost so much and saw Allegra as a replacement for the mother she had lost, a role that she could never fulfill.

Allegra opened the front door. A blonde-haired woman stood behind two police officers.

'Where is she?' the woman demanded.

'Let me deal with this, ma'am,' the police officer said, his name tag identifying him as Officer Sanders. 'We are here seeking Amethyst Revett—'

'You have no right to her,' the woman interjected, cutting off Officer Sanders. 'She's mine.'

Allegra felt a primal urge to hit her in the face. The woman was talking about Amethyst as if she was a belonging and not a child.

'And who are you?' Allegra demanded.

'I am Imogen Revett. Amethyst's aunt and legal guardian.'

Allegra hesitated. A moment ago, she'd wanted nothing more than to pass Amethyst on, get her out of her life, and put away the memories she didn't want. But now that all she had to do was to tell the police officer where Amethyst was, she hesitated. There was something about Imogen that raised Allegra's hackles.

'You have no right to her,' Imogen continued. 'You gave her up. I'm her blood.'

Allegra raised an eyebrow. 'If you're her guardian, then why don't you know where she is?'

'Enough. Officer Hunt, please take Ms Revett out,' Officer Sanders said.

Allegra waited until Imogen left, giving her one last malevolent look over her shoulder.

'I apologize for that. Ms Revett is upset that her ward is missing.' Officer Sanders glanced out the window where Imogen was pacing under the watchful eye of Officer Hunt. 'We're looking for thirteen-year-old Amethyst Revett. She didn't return from school yesterday. I believe you know who that is?'

'Yes, I do. I was friends with her mother, Amy.'

'Do you know where Amethyst is?'

'I do not,' Allegra said, looking at the empty kitchen. Presumably, Amethyst had retreated to the hidey-hole she had discovered within the house. 'How did you know to find me? All the legal arrangements were sealed and not a matter of public record.'

'When Amethyst didn't return home during the night, Ms Revett found her diary. In it, she talks about contacting her birth mother.' He took a business card out of his pocket. 'If she makes contact, please call us.'

'I will,' Allegra said, taking the card in hand.

She escorted Officer Sanders out and watched from the window as Imogen protested, waving her hand at the house, probably insisting that the police search her home. After Office Sanders spoke to her, she reluctantly sat in the police car. Allegra waited until they'd left the driveway before walking up the stairs.

'Amethyst,' she called as she walked. 'They're gone. Come out so we can talk.'

As she walked down the long corridor, she began feeling scared. What if Amethyst had run away and Allegra had placed her in greater danger by not telling the police about her visit? Just when she was about to call 911 and confess everything, Amethyst appeared in a doorway. Allegra took a deep breath, stopping herself from chastising her.

'Is this where you've been staying?' she asked instead as she followed Amethyst back in.

Amethyst nodded her head. The room had a four-poster bed, the fabric moth-eaten and covered with dust. Amethyst pushed open the creaky wardrobe door. It was a walk-in wardrobe, built for a woman with acres of clothes, with broken shelves and a musty smell. Behind the corner was a shoe wardrobe, and Amethyst had set up a makeshift bed on the floor with some old curtains.

'Is this where you slept last night?' Allegra asked, feeling horrible.

'It's not too bad,' Amethyst said. 'I like how cozy it is.'

'Why didn't you talk to me last night?' Allegra asked.

'I fell asleep while I waited for you, and then when I was trying to find you to talk to you, you were so scared. By the time I'd decided to tell you I was here, you left again.'

Allegra felt chagrined. If only she hadn't be-haved like a hysterical woman in a Victorian novel, they could have cleared all this up the night before.

Allegra heard Amethyst's stomach gurgle. 'Let's go eat.' She walked downstairs to the kitchen, acutely aware of Amethyst right behind her.

Allegra made breakfast for her.

'Why did you run away from your aunt?' Allegra asked.

'We had a fight last night. I wanted to tell her about you, but she just didn't want to listen. She never listens to anything I have to say.' Amethyst looked down at the table.

'That might be true, but you still terrified her by running away. She's your family.'

'Not really. I mean, I hardly saw her when my parents were alive, and now she's stuck with me because there's no one else. You're my real family. You're my Mom.'

'There's something I have to tell you,' Allegra started, feeling like she was choking. She did not want to have this conversation. She did not want to see the light and hope leave Amethyst's eyes, but she had to rip this fantasy as quickly as possible. 'I'm not your mother.'

'I know that,' Amethyst said.

'You do?' Allegra said, frowning.

'Of course, Amy was my mom, and you're my birth mother.'

'No, actually I'm not,' Allegra said. 'Amy gave birth to you.'

'But I look exactly like you,' Amethyst looked her up and down. She put her hand out and touched Allegra's hand. 'Even our hands are the same.'

Allegra looked down and felt a chill. She should have known that this was a possibility. That any genetic offspring of hers would dominate the gene pool and ensure that their resemblance was uncanny. After all, she'd poured enough over her mother's photo album, in awe at the resemblance of her grandmother and great-grandmother. It was as if she'd been looking at her mother in a historical costume.

'We look alike because I donated an egg to your parents. They had tried to have a baby for such a long time, but they just couldn't.'

Allegra had known Amy since they were children. When she left home at 18, it was Amy who offered her a job as an assistant, which was a combination of dog-walker and house sitter, while Allegra completed her Bachelor of Arts Degree in Design at the Fashion Institute of Design and Merchandising. Allegra was a trust fund baby, but her mother had spitefully advised the lawyers to change the age when Allegra could access her fund to 36 to force Allegra into submitting to her will, while her adored older brother received his trust fund when he was 18. Her mother thought that she was going to break Allegra into coming home. Instead, all she did was harden Allegra's resolve to not give up on her dream.

Amy and David had been married for twelve years and had been trying to conceive for ten of those years. They'd had three pregnancies that ended with a miscarriage and had four dogs that became their surrogate children and that they lavished all their love and attention on. When Allegra began working for them, the doctor had told them there was no chance that Amy could have a biological child. Her IVF attempts had brought on early menopause, and her fertility was at an end. Their only option now was to get an egg donor.

Allegra was dating Cole, an aspiring musician trying to make it with his rock band. They both had stars in their eyes. Allegra wanted to start her own fashion label and was doing the yards of creating her first collection for a college show. She was house-sitting while Amy and David had a weekend getaway to celebrate their anniversary. Cole stayed over, and in the morning, she found him in the study going through the fertility clinic profiles for potential egg donors. All the profiles were for women with Amy's dark hair coloring and blue eyes.

'All that searching and you're a dead ringer,' Cole said.

She'd told him about the embarrassing incident the other day when David came into the kitchen while Allegra was putting dishes in the dishwasher and embraced her, thinking she was his wife. He'd been mortified, and they'd never spoken of it. Allegra had gone to the hairdresser the same day and had her waist-length hair cut to her shoulders so there wouldn't be a repeat.

Cole whistled as he held up a piece of paper. It was the donor contract, a non-disclosure agreement stating the fee to cover medical expenses and inconvenience. 'Being a donor sure is a lucrative gig. You should do it?' he said with a comical waggle of his eyebrows.

Allegra laughed. She'd thought that was the end of the conversation, but then everything changed when Cole left his band and desperately needed money for equipment to set himself up as a solo artist. He'd told her the guitarist pushed him out because he wanted to be the lead singer. She didn't realize until afterward that he was a gambler and had been wasting all his money. All she knew at the time was that he was the love of her life, and she would do anything to make him happy.

When he first proposed that she donate an egg, she reacted violently and rejected him on the spot. They'd already had the talk about children, and he knew she never wanted any kids. Her mother had subjected her to too much bad parenting to ever want to pass that inheritance on.

'That's why this is perfect. You're not having a child, but you're leaving a legacy. This money could be our big break, our chance to make it with no one holding us back.'

She had exhibited her designs at the college fashion show but hadn't won first prize. Her fashion designs were viewed as too out there. She desperately wanted to move on with her life and prove to her mother, who vehemently disapproved of her career choice, that she could be successful. Once Cole put the idea there, it had festered and grown, and then when she saw Amy crying after a visit from her best friend who had three children, Allegra knew she wanted to help her.

So she'd agreed, but there had been a part of her flinching at the thought. Everything had gone as planned. Her eggs were harvested, and the doctors performed the IVF procedure with David's sperm. They transferred the embryos to Amy, and the pregnancy progressed.

Life should have been perfect. She'd helped a friend, she was in love, and she and Cole finally had money to make their dreams come true. Except that within two months, Cole had gambled her money away, and Amy distanced herself from Allegra after she fell pregnant and eventually fired her, softening the blow by referring her to another friend of hers. Allegra didn't blame Amy. She knew Amy wanted a chance to forget that the baby was anything other than her child. Allegra had her own reasons for leaving. She wanted to forget that she had broken her vow to bring a baby into the world.

Every once in a while, she dreamed about Amy as she last saw her, standing at the crib in the baby nursery she had completed. In her dream, Amy beckoned her to come and look in the crib at the baby, but when Allegra approached, the crib was always empty. Amy's smiling face transformed into a look of terror, and she screamed at Allegra, 'What did you do?'

Allegra shook off the memories and took a deep breath. 'I donated the egg, and it was fertilized with your father's sperm, and then you were implanted in your mother's womb. All we share is a genetic code, but we're not related.'

As she looked at Amethyst, her heart cried. Amethyst was David's biological child, and Allegra could faintly see him in Amethyst's forehead and eyebrows, but otherwise, it was as if his genetic code was wiped from the process.

'So you don't think I'm related to you.' Amethyst blinked back tears. 'God, I have no one.'

'That's not true. You have your aunt. She is your relative. She's your Dad's sister,' Allegra said, making her voice brisk to hide the fact that she was at breaking point.

'But she doesn't understand me. Everything I do is wrong. Everything about me is wrong. I don't think she even likes me.'

'Of course she does. She loves you. She just might not know how to show it.' Allegra felt a sense of déja vu as she spoke. She was shaken as she realized that she'd heard these words before. They were what her father had told her to comfort her after yet another fight with her mother.

Allegra took the police officer's business card and dialed. 'I'm going to call your aunt.'

Amethyst sat at the table, her food uneaten. She didn't cry, but her shoulders were bent as if she was carrying a heavy weight. She looked defeated. Allegra tried to initiate conversation while they waited, but Amethyst just nodded yes or no, her face vacant.

The police returned, Imogen not far behind.

'I was surprised to receive your phone call,' Officer Sanders said. 'I thought you said that Amethyst didn't make any contact.'

'She didn't. She squatted here last night,' Allegra said.

Imogen waited outside and ran to hug Amethyst when she walked out. Amethyst clutched her aunt's waist briefly before letting her arms hang limply by her side. Imogen kept her arm around Amethyst's shoulders as they walked to the car but didn't speak. Amethyst didn't look back at the house once.

Allegra stepped away from the window when the car disappeared from the driveway and covered her face with her hands. Why did she feel as if she did the wrong thing? She wasn't Amethyst's relative and had no right to her.

Allegra stood at the window, her thoughts drifting like leaves on a gentle breeze. Memories danced before her, their edges softened by time. Then, through the veil of nostalgia, she spotted a car approaching. Her heart quickened as recognition dawned—it was Emmett. She checked her watch and sighed inwardly; she had completely forgotten their date.

Chapter 4

Emmett couldn't take his eyes off Allegra as she gracefully descended the stairs. She seemed like a character straight out of a Golden Age movie, a timeless beauty who had stepped off the silver screen and into his life. A sense of inadequacy washed over him in her presence, making him feel gauche.

'Care for a drink?' Allegra inquired, gliding over to a drinks cart against the wall.

He glanced at his watch. 'No, we're going to be late for our reservation.'

Allegra hesitated, her radiant smile faltering momentarily. 'I'm sorry I was late. I had a few surprises today.'

'No, it's fine,' Emmett assured her, though he couldn't help but feel flustered. He was swept along in the whirlwind of her presence.

After locking her front door, he held the car door open for her. As he walked to the driver's seat, he couldn't help but feel like an awkward teenager again, stumbling over his words. Being near her had a way of regressing him to a time when he dreamed of a girlfriend but couldn't quite make it happen.

'So, you said you had some surprises today?' he asked, trying to break the silence that had fallen between them. 'Did that have something to do with the police cars leaving your driveway as I pulled up?' He'd been waiting for an opportunity to ask. She'd greeted him at the door flustered, telling him she was running late, and he'd spent half an hour cooling his heels downstairs as he waited for her to get ready.

'Oh, nothing worth talking about. What about your day?' she inquired.

His hands tightened on the steering wheel. Just as he began hoping that Virginia was wrong in estimating her character, Allegra's evasion showed him she was a liar involved in some dicey things. He was right to be helping Virginia to uncover her duplicitousness.

'It was good,' Emmett replied.

Allegra nodded, and an uncomfortable silence settled in the car. Emmett turned on the radio, eager to dispel the tension, but the sudden blast of rap music took them both by surprise. 'Sorry about that,' he quickly changed the station.

'I wouldn't have taken you for a rap fan?' she asked.

'I'm not. My previous passenger,' he replied, avoiding any mention of Rhys at this early stage of their date.

She looked at him questioningly, but he didn't elaborate.

Emmett pulled up in front of the restaurant a few minutes later, still feeling slightly out of his element.

As the maitre d' led them to their table, Emmett couldn't help but notice the stares from other patrons. Heads turned as they walked by, and while Allegra maintained a regal composure, her subtle smile of pleasure didn't go unnoticed. Emmett felt like he was on display and found it disconcerting.

'You're quite the head-turner,' he commented after they were seated.

'You say that like it's a bad thing,' Allegra replied, arching an eyebrow.

'No, no, of course not,' Emmett stammered. 'I just meant that your outfit is very attention-grabbing.'

'This is just what I wear. I love vintage fashion.'

'Well, it suits you,' Emmett said, his eyes lingering on her.

'I don't wear it just for the looks. I love finding a piece of clothing that's existed for years and re-stitching and mending it, giving it a whole new lease of life. It brings me joy to take something secondhand and give it a new life and purpose. We're so caught up in a consumer culture that it's just about surrounding ourselves with things for the sake of it, rather than having things that are beautiful and feed our soul.'

As Allegra spoke, her face lit up with passion, and Emmett found himself drawn into her excitement. 'I know what you mean. I think we're too quick to favor new over old, to assume that only new things have value and anything old doesn't.'

She smiled at him, and his earlier awkwardness seemed to melt away. 'So, what's your passion?' she asked.

'My job keeps me busy,' he admitted. 'What about you?'

'I love fashion. I worked as a costume designer on a soap opera, and now I design for my clients. So, my job and passion are one and the same.' She smiled at the waiter as he served their drinks and took a sip. 'What's your specialty?' Allegra inquired, her ruby-red lips glistening.

Emmett had to tear his gaze away from her lips to meet her eyes. 'Intellectual property lawyer,' he lied. He was here on a mission, and to do that, he had to be undercover.

'Oh,' Allegra responded, her tone tinged with bemusement. 'So, you're passionate about intellectual law.'

'You sound like you don't approve?' Emmett said, feeling a bit exposed by her reaction.

'No, no,' she quickly reassured him. 'I guess it takes all kinds.'

'I impress most people with my credentials,' Emmett stated, finding it an unfamiliar sensation to be met with skepticism about his profession.

'I'm not most people,' Allegra replied, leaning back in her chair and taking another sip.

'No, you certainly aren't,' he agreed, his gaze lingering on her. Her porcelain skin seemed to glow, and he couldn't help but wonder what it would be like to kiss her neck.

Their eyes locked, and he blushed as he saw the awareness in her gaze. She knew exactly how she affected him. The waiter arrived to take their order, saving him from the intense moment.

'What about dancing?' Emmett asked after the waiter left. 'Isn't that another passion?'

'Yes, it is, but a more recent one,' Allegra confessed.

'What made you take up dancing?' he inquired, curious about her journey.

Allegra hesitated. 'I went through a bit of a transformation. Started re-evaluating my life's prospects,' she replied with a bright smile, leaning in closer.

He took a deep breath as her cleavage tantalizingly spilled from her dress. 'Sounds like there's a story there,' he ventured.

'Maybe,' Allegra repeated, her eyes sparkling with mischief.

Their waiter appeared with their drinks, and Emmett flushed as he averted his gaze.

'Do you enjoy being an intellectual lawyer?'

'Not really.' He didn't know if it was being honest because all the blood had rushed out of his head or because he knew she wasn't impressed with his job. 'I wanted to be an environmental lawyer, but it didn't work out.'

'Why not?' she asked.

'My father had other plans for me.'

He remembered how his father had forbidden him from studying what he considered "airy fairy." He had the Dennison family name to uphold. It was only a few months before that 5-year-old Rhys was diagnosed with autism, and his father was reeling from the threat to his family legacy now that he only had one son to rely on.

Emmett might have fought his father and taken on the inevitable fallout of being disinherited and having to take out a study loan to pay his way through college, but he couldn't do it to his mother. While he would be away at college and away from the firing line, she was the one who remained behind and endured his father's cutting jibes. He already blamed her for one defective son. If Emmett followed his dream, it would just be another black mark against his mother for supposedly 'indulging him too much.'

'And do you always do what your father says?'
Allegra asked. Her voice held a teasing note.

He forced a smile. 'Not anymore.' He tipped
the wineglass to his lips and sipped.

Allegra looked at him with concern. 'And what
about your parents?' he asked, trying to steer
the conversation toward less charged territory.

'Oh, my parents did not want me to be a fashion designer. They wanted me to be something
more respectable, like a lawyer,' Allegra said
with a playful glint in her eye.

Emmett laughed. 'Touché.' He raised his glass
to toast her.

There was a lull in the conversation, and he
wondered how to get the conversation to her
dating life and Henry.

'Is this a restaurant you bring all your dates
to?' Allegra asked.

He couldn't believe his luck. She was doing his
job for him.

'No,' he cleared his throat. 'I was in a long-term
relationship and haven't dated for a while. This
restaurant was recommended in an article I
read.'

'How long were you together for?'

He didn't want to answer. Any memories of his
fiancé brought up bitterness and resentment.
Allegra was waiting for an answer.

'Two years,' he finally admitted. 'We broke up
a year ago.' He twirled the wineglass, his eyes

caught on the crystal sparkling under the light. 'I thought we were perfectly matched in every way: same interests, same profession, same passion.' He laughed wryly. 'But I was wrong. She found someone more suited.' He took a sip. 'And you?'

'No, no one serious.'

'Never?' he prodded.

'Someone a long time ago, but since then, I like to keep it light and breezy. No commitment, no hurt feelings.'

He knew she was warning him away, and disappointment burned within him. Even though he knew this wasn't an actual date, he'd wanted something more. Something real and true.

'What about the man you inherited the mansion from? I thought you were together?' Emmett asked boldly, his fingers gripping the glass stem.

'Henry was a friend. My best friend.'

'Wasn't he older?' Emmett prodded.

'How do you...'

'I mean, he passed away, so I'm assuming he was older,' he quickly added.

Allegra's bewildered expression cleared, and he had an internal sigh of relief for covering up his misstep.

'He was older, yes, but that wasn't how he died. He had cancer. We bonded over our mutual love of dancing and spent a lot of time together, purely platonic.' Allegra held up a hand. 'He was firmly in love with his wife, and even though he'd been a widower for a few years, he always said she was his one true love.'

Allegra's smile was tender. 'They had the real thing, and when he died, he looked so happy as he called her name. I know that they're reunited.' Allegra had a tear slowly drifting down her face.

This wasn't the story Virginia told him. She'd said that Henry died from a heart attack and that Allegra had seduced him, tricking him into getting engaged so that he would include her in his will. He frowned, attempting to clear his mind.

'Didn't he have family to leave the mansion to?' he asked.

Allegra nodded. 'His niece, he left her the land and the mansion to me.'

'Oh,' Emmett said, his head spinning. This was definitely not the story that Virginia had told him. According to her, Allegra inherited the entire property, including the land and the mansion. While the mansion and the land it was on were worth millions of dollars, it was a modest sum compared to the acres of land worth ten times that.

He wanted to ask more questions but realized she would misconstrue it as him being a gold-digger. Anyway, it wasn't up to Allegra to answer any more questions. He needed to speak to Virginia and get to the truth.

As the evening wore on, they flirted and enjoyed each other's company. Emmett found himself thoroughly enchanted, forgetting this was supposed to be a pretend date. After he paid the bill, they strolled toward the car park. As they drove past the Hot Spot, he couldn't help but smile, recalling their first encounter.

Allegra was looking out the window when she gasped. 'Stop here,' she said, her voice filled with urgency.

Emmett stopped the car. 'What's wrong?'

'I saw something in the alley. It looks like Joleen,' Allegra exclaimed, opening her door and running.

Emmett glanced at his rearview mirror, relieved that there were no other vehicles, and parked on the curb. He quickly followed Allegra. She was determined, despite her high heels, while Emmett's marathon runner legs easily closed the gap.

When they reached the end of the alley, the sound of breaking glass and shouting reached their ears.

'That sounds like Joleen,' Allegra said, her voice fraught with worry.

Emmett urged caution, shouting, 'Stop, we have to call the police.' He reached for his phone, but Allegra was already halfway down the alley.

'Damnit,' he muttered, returning his phone to his pocket and sprinting after her.

As they turned the corner, they witnessed Joleen struggling with two men. One of them had her firmly by the arms, while the other was viciously punching her. The hate-filled slurs they spewed made Emmett's blood boil.

'Stop it, you homophobic pricks!' Allegra shouted as she launched herself at one attacker, climbing onto his back.

'Hey, get off!' the man grunted as he tried to shake her off, but Allegra clung on tenaciously.

The other man released Joleen, who fell to the ground, gasping for breath. Emmett watched in horror as the situation escalated.

Emmett turned to see the man Allegra was fighting had knocked her off his back and was holding her by the neck.

Emmett ran at him, hitting him in the torso with his head and grabbing him around the waist. The force of Emmett's run-up sent the man flying away from Allegra. He started punching Emmett, trying to force him to let go. Emmett held tight to his waist, grunting with pain as the bruising punches continued. He couldn't let go so he could hurt Allegra. Suddenly, the man who had been attacking Allegra fell to the ground, incapacitated. Emmett blinked in surprise, and then he saw Joleen, armed with a plank of wood, standing behind the fallen assailant.

Emmett returned his attention to the man who had been fighting him. The man let out a string of curses and continued to punch Emmett, trying to force him to release his hold. Emmett refused to let go. Then, he felt reinforcements - Allegra kicked the man, and Joleen used the plank to strike him.

The assailant finally fell, and Emmett could release him. As they all caught their breath, they heard the distant sound of sirens approaching.

'Shit, we've got to get out of here,' one attacker declared, helping his wounded companion to his feet, and they fled down the alley.

'Should we go after them?' Emmett asked, still panting and nursing his bruises.

'No need,' Joleen said, triumphantly displaying a wallet she had taken from one attacker. 'Those cowards can run, but they can't hide.'

They heard sirens. Emmett felt relief fill him. The police were on its way. Emmett looked at Allegra with admiration, seeing a strength in her that was truly awe-inspiring. He'd set out on a date with the woman that Virginia had told him about, who used her sexual allure to manipulate men into complying with her underhanded motives, but he was now realizing that this was a fabrication. This was the real Allegra, a woman who was willing to throw herself in the path of danger to protect a friend.

He realized that this pretend-date had become all too real during dinner and the fight, and he was falling hard.

Chapter 5

Allegra stood next to Joleen while the police took her statement. A paramedic was examining Emmett. He took off his shirt, wincing as he lifted his arm. He was wearing a white singlet underneath. His body was toned and lithe, just the way she liked it. The police lights lit up the back of the café, and it caught Emmett in its neon glow. The paramedic lifted his white singlet, showing his six-pack, and pressed on his ribs.

Allegra was surprised by his muscly body. He didn't look like a nerd now, wearing only a singlet, his hair disarrayed, and his face scowling. As she watched him, she felt herself getting aroused. Well, this was a surprise. She'd thought after their date that he was a pleasant man. There had been some sparks, but she was unsure whether she should pursue it. He struck her as the hearts and flowers type, and she was strictly into fun and flirty.

Allegra dragged her eyes away and focused on the conversation between Joleen and the police officer.

'Have you seen the suspects before?' the police officer asked.

'He was in the café earlier,' Joleen said. 'He and his mate were sniggering and called me a lady man. Made some stupid remark about me taking my wife's wardrobe. When I came out to take the garbage, they were waiting for me. One of them grabbed me and the other started hitting into me before I had a chance to take a breath. If it was one-on-one I would have knocked them out. I've had enough practice.'

The police officer looked up and down Joleen's six-foot frame and nodded.

Joleen handed over the wallet. 'This fell out of his pocket.'

The police officer lifted his eyebrow but said nothing. He opened the wallet and pulled out the license. 'This might help us with our inquiries. There has been a spate of homophobic attacks. We'll be in touch for a follow-up.'

The police officer walked back to the squad car.

Allegra's eyes kept returning to Emmett. The paramedic was packing up, and Emmett pulled his t-shirt back down his stomach. He looked at her, and their eyes caught. He looked transformed. Gone was the mild-mannered man she'd met. In his place was a man with his blood heated.

'Easy girl,' Joleen said in her ear. 'You look like you're going to eat him up.'

Allegra bit her lip. 'I might.'

Joleen looked him over too and smiled. 'He does look tasty.'

Joleen started walking, and Allegra noticed she was barefoot. Her shoes had come off during the struggle. Allegra collected Joleen's high heels and helped her put them on. 'Thank you, darling,' Joleen said, fixing her wig. She took out her vanity and looked at herself. 'Oh, that ain't pretty.'

'You're always beautiful,' Allegra said.

Joleen put away her vanity and met her eyes. 'Thank you, gorgeous,' she said, tearing up.

Allegra hugged her friend and began walking with her. 'Come on, let's get you home.'

Emmett walked over.

'What's the damage?' Allegra asked.

'Just some bruising,' Emmett said. 'Nothing to worry about.' There was a dark bruise forming on his cheekbone. 'What about the two of you?' he asked.

'I'm all right,' Allegra said, even though she could still feel the thug's grasping hands squeezing her windpipe. She knew there would be a bruise there in the morning.

'I've taken a stronger whooping than that from my younger sister,' Joleen said, putting her strut on as she sashayed down the alley.

'Thanks for your help,' Allegra said as Emmett stepped in beside her.

'No problems.' Emmett took her hand in his.

'I'm going to get Joleen home.'

'I'll give you both a lift,' Emmett said.

'Thanks.' Allegra squeezed his hand. She liked the feeling of him walking beside her. She felt protected and cherished.

They took Joleen to her house, and Allegra walked her friend inside while Emmett waited by the car. 'I'll go say goodbye to Emmett and stay with you tonight,' Allegra said as she saw the way Joleen was wincing with pain. She'd crashed on Joleen's couch a time or two when they went clubbing together.

'It's all right.' Joleen took off her wig and placed it on the coffee table. 'You go on home. I need some downtime by myself.'

She looked so despondent sitting there that Allegra leaned down and hugged Joleen, holding her against her side. Allegra knew from past conversations that this wasn't the first time that Joleen had been attacked, and while she put on a brave front about it, violence took its toll.

'Are you sure?' Allegra asked.

Joleen tipped her head back and met her eyes. For a moment, Joleen vanished and Allegra saw

Joe, Joleen's alter-ego. 'I'm fine,' Joe said, his voice deeper and rougher than Joleen's.

Allegra realized Joleen was shaken up and needed time to process with no one around. 'Okay.' She leaned down and kissed Joleen on the forehead.

'You take that man of yours home and give him a proper thank you.' Joleen pushed her away gently.

Allegra laughed through her tears. It was what she was thinking, after all.

When she got out, Emmett was waiting on the sidewalk for her. She felt suddenly shy as she approached him.

'How is she?' Emmett asked.

'Putting on a brave face,' Allegra said.

Emmett held the door open for her. After she sat down, he closed the door and walked around. He'd put his shirt back on but hadn't done up the buttons, and the shirt tails flapped against his side. He sat in the driver's seat, and she stole a look at him. The singlet was skin tight, and she could see every ridge of his muscled torso. As he drove, she was aware of his body next to hers. His hands were on the wheel, the knuckles grazed, and she remembered how he'd hit the thug. He'd been so heroic, throwing himself into the fray to save her without a thought about his safety.

He stopped at her house and came around to open the door.

'That looks bruised.' She gently placed her hand on his cheek. He held himself still under her hand. 'You should come in and ice it.'

His eyes were wide and full of questions. She took his hand and led him inside.

She sat him on the couch and got a bag of peas. 'This will help,' she said, sitting beside him and holding the bag against his face.

He put his hand over hers, and their eyes caught. She leaned in and kissed him. His lips were hesitant and unsure under hers. She felt her excitement build. The paradox of his rough looks and then the uncertainty with which he kissed her was a turn-on like no other. Usually, the men she was in were quick and rushed, and it was the way she liked it.

She sat on his lap, holding his arms down as she kissed him hard. He pushed back, taking hold of her hands and putting them behind her back. He held her gently, without hurting her, but she was aware of his strength. It surprised her how easily he took control, but even though her breasts were arching toward his face, he didn't pursue them. His lips made their way from her lips to her neck and shoulders. She tilted her head back in surprise, looking up at the ceiling above them as she felt his lips on her arms, his fingertips tracing her waist gently.

She was confused. She wanted the rush of lust, the burst of passion where she was swept away by the needs of her body and couldn't think. As Emmett gently caressed her, she felt cherished. She thought about her body and what it had been subjected to as the doctors treated her for cancer. The chemotherapy that made her wish for death, the radiotherapy that made her skin tender and sore, the tablets for pain relief and nausea that made her stomach churn inside out. It felt like Emmett was gently kissing away the pain, and it brought tears to her eyes.

She pushed his hands away and yanked off his singlet, her hands smoothing down his chest until she reached his fly. She lifted herself onto her knees as she pulled his zipper down, her hand grasping for his erection.

'No.' He took her hand away. 'I want to go slow.'

He dragged her hands back around his neck and kissed her, holding her tightly against his bare chest. She felt herself crumbling under his tenderness. Allegra didn't ever remember being in a moment like this. She teared up and fell off his lap. 'Sorry, sorry,' she said, covering her face.

'It's okay.' Emmett kissed her shoulder and pulled her against his side, his arm over her shoulder. 'You were just attacked. Of course you're feeling shaken up.'

'It's not that. I'm just not feeling like myself.' She peeked at him, wondering how he would take it. His concerned eyes were steady on hers. 'I had breast cancer.'

'I'm so sorry.' He reached over and caressed her hair. 'Are you okay?'

'Yes, I'm in remission. I'm still coming to terms with it.' Emmett was the first potential lover that she'd told. Even though she'd had other lovers, she had told none of them about her illness. It had somehow felt too intimate, yet telling Emmett felt so natural and effortless. 'It changed my whole life.'

It has been a shock when she discovered the lump in her left breast. Her first instinct was to deny it, pretend it wasn't happening. It was only after she woke up in a cold sweat after a one-week bender of alcohol and messy sex and faced the fact that she was risking her life that she went to see her doctor.

Her doctor's face had creased with concern as soon as he touched her breast. The x-ray results didn't take long. It was definitely breast cancer. By the end of that week, she had begun therapy.

Emmett helped her sit up in bed. 'I met my best friend Henry while I was in treatment.'

She'd noticed Henry during her first treatment. He'd been a dapper gentleman wearing a retro suit and Fedora hat and had looked like he'd stepped out of a 1950s catalog. When he'd attempted to catch her eye, she kept her gaze clamped to the iPad she carried to distract her, not in the mood for company. He didn't let that put him off.

'I'm reading the books first,' he said, holding up a Game of Thrones book.

Allegra had nodded, but she didn't make eye contact.

'You're probably thinking I'm an old man hitting on the hot young chick,' he said, reading her mind. 'But this is more of a case of a sick man needing a distraction.'

He disarmed her by making jokes about the hospital and cancer. Soon, she was talking to him, and not long after that, she was looking out for him. He made the time go faster, and most importantly, he was the only one who understood what she was going through. She had shared news of her illness with some of her 'friends,' and that's when she found out their true character. Her so-called friends were uncomfortable with the fact that she was sick. Most of them responded with some gesture, a bouquet, some chocolates, but nobody really understood the realities of what she needed.

She needed a shoulder to cry on when the illness knocked her about, and she started wondering if the nausea and illness were worth it and that perhaps death would be a welcome relief from her suffering. Allegra needed home-cooked meals so that she could heat food when she wasn't feeling well. She needed people to call and check on her, see how she was going, and prove to her that life was worth living, but most of them disappeared.

The only one who gave her any genuine support was Maree, but the twins occupied her attention. Maree came and stayed with her overnight during each treatment and always made sure that she left frozen meals in the freezer, but Allegra felt like she couldn't burden her with the darkness of her thoughts and moods.

'Henry was the one who listened to me. He had the time, and he understood the toll that a life-threatening illness took on someone's psyche,' she told Emmett.

Soon, they started meeting up outside of hospital, and then there was the day that he changed her life. He invited her to his dancing class, where they danced the Salsa, merengue, Cha Cha, Rumba, and Samba. While to her, these had been retro dances, to Henry, they were much-loved dances he grew up with. For once, she had blended right in with her love of vintage fashion. Everyone dressed as if they came from another decade, and she finally realized why she and Henry were such kindred spirits.

'Henry taught me how to dance, but he did so much more. He helped me find a new lease on life,' she told Emmett, not adding that she felt reborn after her illness. Before her diagnosis, she felt like she had been drifting from man to man. She'd always had a vague dream of incorporating her love of vintage into a passion, but there had always been something else to do. She'd thought she had all the time in the world until she didn't. After her illness, she wanted to do something amazing and leave a legacy.

She and Henry bonded over his love of dancing, and soon, the jitterbug caught Allegra. Henry took her to his home and showed her Eagle's Ridge. It was his ancestral home that his great-grandfather, a 1930s matinee movie actor, had started and subsequent generations had added to, but that had fallen into disrepair over the years. Homes like that needed significant capital for the upkeep, and Henry's family fell into hard times. Henry had lived in the pool house behind the property, unable to find the capital for renovations.

'I'm out of time,' he told Allegra as he showed her around and told her about his dream to bring the house back to glory and to re-make it into a grand dance hall that offered dance classes and was used as a regular social hall.

'Even though I have shaken off the cancer, I don't have the time or the money to do this house proud. But you do. I want you to have her when I'm gone. I want you to take my dream over.'

Henry was one of the few people who knew everything about her, including who her parents were, but she didn't tell Emmett that. She could only share that secret when she was sure someone was truly interested in her.

As she walked through the ballroom, her high heels clacking on the worn and faded floorboards, she fell in love with the Art Deco ceiling plaster domes and roses. She pictured how the ballroom would look when it was restored. Resplendent crystal chandeliers hanging from the restored ceiling like a diamond necklace hanging from the neck of a beautiful woman. How the soft light would light up the ceiling roses and shimmer off the polished floorboards, as dancers' shoes clacked on the floorboards. She could almost hear the music and laughter as the house came to life again. It was as if the house was calling to her, speaking to her about times gone by and begging her to take her on.

'You can hear her,' Henry said. 'You can hear the old girl.'

Allegra looked away, not wanting him to think she was crazy.

'Don't worry, my family was ready to put me into a nursing home. They called me crazy for talking about the house as if she was real, but you and I know different.'

They were standing out the front of the house now. As Allegra admired the Queen Anne-style house, she felt she'd finally found her home. She was scared at how much she wanted her.

'He was the one I inherited the mansion from.' She wiped a tear as she remembered Henry and the way the days spent together undergoing treatment had transformed her life.

'Didn't he have family?' Emmett asked.

'A niece.' Allegra said. She'd met Virginia once when she dropped in to check on Henry. She'd watched Allegra with suspicion when Henry had introduced her as his friend and didn't elaborate on their connection to protect Allegra's privacy.

When she'd asked Henry the same thing, he shook his head. 'Virginia comes around for the obligatory visit, just pretending to do her duty so I don't forget her in my will, but I know what she is up to. I caught a surveyor on the property the other day. He was working for her husband, and they were sizing up the land. They thought I was at the hospital for chemo. They didn't know I had re-scheduled so I could be with you. I'll leave her the land at the back, and you can have the old girl.'

The back of the house was once stately gardens that had descended into a tangled mess, and the land was probably worth more than the house itself.

'Henry was still completely loyal to his family and ensured Virginia received the true inheritance. He just knew that she would want to tear down the mansion and exploit these few acres too, and he couldn't stand for that to happen.'

Allegra felt relaxed and happy, unburdened now that she'd told Emmett the truth. She leaned down and kissed him. He gently kissed her and tugged her so she lay her head on his shoulder.

'That's okay,' Emmett said. 'I've got all the time in the world.'

She knew she should get up and walk him out, end this strange night, but it was so nice to be leaning on his strength. The night had been so far out of her comfort zone. Allegra was used to being with men who were only interested in one thing and were ruled by their physical desire, yet Emmett had rejected her. She should worry that she was losing her feminine allure, yet instead, she felt more valued and precious than she'd ever felt before. The pull of fatigue worked its way through her. She would get up in a moment and walk Emmett out.

Chapter 6

Emmett lay in the dimly lit room, his gaze fixed on the ceiling as he tried to decipher the tangled web of deceit he had woven. Beside him, Allegra was sleeping peacefully, her rhythmic breathing serving as a soothing melody in the night's quiet. Moonlight filtered through the curtains, casting a gentle glow on her features, and Emmett couldn't help but be captivated by her serene beauty.

He had been dishonest with Allegra, feigning interest in her while secretly spying on her every move to uncover information that could jeopardize her inheritance. Emmett had been convinced that his friend Virginia's claims about Allegra were accurate, that she had somehow manipulated her way into inheriting the mansion, but now he knew there was more to it than what Virginia had let him to believe. Allegra and Henry had both had cancer, undergone cancer treatment together. Their connection wasn't romantic, but one forged through the heartbreak of surviving death, and Virginia had received the land.

As he lay there beside her, watching her delicate form in slumber, he couldn't deny the tangled emotions swirling within him. What had started as a mission to gather evidence had evolved into something much deeper. He had fallen for Allegra, and the guilt of his deception weighed heavily on his conscience.

Gently, Emmett reached out and brushed a strand of hair away from Allegra's peaceful face. Her lips curved into a soft smile even in her sleep, and he marveled at the genuine warmth he saw in her expression. She was nothing like the conniving, manipulative woman Virginia had led him to believe she was.

In the night's stillness, Emmett contemplated the choices he had made. He had never intended to become emotionally entangled with Allegra. It had been a means to an end, a path to uncover the truth about the mansion's inheritance. But now, his heart was torn between his loyalty toward Virginia and his undeniable connection with Allegra.

As he lay there, the weight of his deception bearing down on him, Emmett realized that he had lost sight of what truly mattered. The mansion, the inheritance, the secrets—they all seemed insignificant compared to the woman beside him. Allegra had unwittingly stolen his heart, and he couldn't bear to continue deceiving her.

With a sigh, Emmett made a difficult decision. He would confront Virginia, demand the truth, and end the web of lies that had entangled him. No matter the consequences, he couldn't let Allegra be hurt by his actions any longer.

Turning his gaze back to Allegra, he brushed his fingers gently across her cheek. She stirred slightly, her eyelashes fluttering open as she looked up at him with drowsy eyes.

'Emmett?' she murmured, her voice laced with sleep.

He smiled down at her, unable to deny the feelings that had taken root in his heart. 'Allegra,' he whispered, 'there's something I need to tell you.'

In that tender moment, Emmett made a silent promise to himself that he would do whatever it took to protect and cherish the woman who had unwittingly become the love of his life, and that meant unraveling the web of deception he had woven around them.

Just then, his phone rang. He lifted the screen and saw it was Betty. 'What's wrong?' he asked when he answered. After the attack, he'd called Rhys and Betty and arranged for his brother to stay the night.

'Rhys had an asthma attack.'

'I'll be right there.' He put on his shirt and trousers. 'I'm sorry. I have an emergency and have to go.'

Allegra frowned, getting up and quickly putting on a red flowing chiffon robe over her silk neglige, and slipped her feet into the low-heeled, open-toed sandals by the bed. 'Okay.' She followed him down the stairs.

'I don't have time to explain now. I'll call you later.'

She nodded and locked the door behind him. He knew he'd made a mess of things, guilt clenching in his gut, and he realized his hypocrisy. She'd opened up and told him all about her cancer treatment, and he'd hidden the most fundamental part of himself, about being a carer for Rhys either. He'd make it up to her.

When he got to Betty's, she opened the door. Rhys was sitting on the couch, clutching his backpack, his face blank.

'He's better now,' Betty's voice was full of concern.

'Thank you,' Emmett sighed, pushing away his resentment. Since he'd become Rhys' carer, his life wasn't his own. He was constantly on call.

As he drove Rhys home, he couldn't help but feel that maybe it was a good thing he and Allegra were interrupted. He had to tell her the truth before they took their relationship to the next level, and before that could happen, he had to confront Virginia.

***

The next afternoon, he met Virginia in a quiet, upscale café, away from prying eyes and curious ears. He'd spent the day with Rhys, playing video games and making sure there were no after-effects from his asthma attack, and he was at home with Betty supervising him.

As he sat across from Virginia at a corner table, the café's ambiance seemed to intensify the tension between them.

'Virginia,' he began, his voice calm but determined, 'we need to talk.'

Virginia, sipping her latte and looking impeccably composed, raised an eyebrow. 'Emmett, darling, what's on your mind?'

Emmett leaned forward, his expression serious. 'It's about Allegra,' he said, choosing his words carefully. 'I need to know the truth, Virginia.'

She set down her coffee cup, a faint smile playing on her lips. 'What truth are you talking about, dear?'

Emmett couldn't help but feel a twinge of frustration at her evasive response. He had always trusted Virginia, but now he was doubting her motivations. 'Don't play games with me, Virginia. You told me that Allegra was a gold-digger, that she manipulated your uncle to secure her spot in the will. Is that true?'

Virginia's smile faded as she realized the gravity of the situation. She glanced around, ensuring no one was listening in on their conversation, before leaning closer to Emmett. 'Of course. I didn't lie.'

Emmett sat across from Virginia in the dimly lit café, the soft hum of conversation and the aroma of freshly brewed coffee filling the air. The tension between them was palpable, and he couldn't avoid the confrontation any longer.

'You didn't tell me they met while they were undergoing cancer treatment together,' he said, his voice tight with frustration.

Virginia looked shocked, her eyes wide with a mixture of surprise and guilt. She fidgeted with the corner of her napkin, her fingers trembling.

'You didn't know,' Emmett pressed, his tone growing sharper.

She shook her head, unable to meet his gaze. The café's ambiance seemed to close in on them as the weight of her deception hung in the air.

'You didn't know your own uncle had cancer and was in treatment. I thought the two of you were close. You said he was your favorite uncle,' Emmett continued, his disappointment evident.

Virginia's shoulders slumped, and she averted her eyes, her hands crumpling the napkin into a small, wrinkled ball.

'He left the mansion to Allegra so it wouldn't be torn down. He wanted it restored,' Emmett said, his frustration battling against his empathy for her.

'That eyesore needs to go. It's a waste of space,' Virginia retorted, her voice tinged with irritation. 'Besides, Allegra got the mansion using deception. She doesn't have the money to restore it.'

'You don't know that?' Emmett said.

'I do. I investigated, and she doesn't have that kind of money.'

'That's beside the point. You got millions' worth of land,' Emmett countered, his patience wearing thin. 'You lied and told me she inherited everything.'

'Yes, but Mike doesn't know that I don't own the mansion. He's spent thousands developing plans, and now if I have to tell him the truth, he'll be angry with me,' Virginia confessed, her eyes glistening with tears.

Emmett recognized this tactic. It was the same ploy she had used to manipulate him into investigating Allegra. But he would not fall for it again.

'Then you're going to have to tell him, and I'm going to tell Allegra the truth,' Emmett declared, his resolve unwavering.

'No, please, give me a few more days,' Virginia pleaded desperately.

Emmett's jaw tightened as he sipped the last of his water, the glass trembling slightly in his hand. He couldn't allow Virginia to control the narrative any longer. It was time for the truth to come out.

Desperation flashed across Virginia's face as she grabbed hold of his arm. 'Please, Emmett,' she implored, her voice trembling with remorse. 'I'm sorry. I'm just desperate. Just give me some time to tell Mike the truth.'

Emmett nodded without looking at her, his decision made. He couldn't let Virginia's desperation lead him astray any longer. He stood up and left the café, the scent of coffee and the murmurs of the patrons fading into the background as he walked away. As soon as he reached the car, he called Allegra and arranged a date.

***

On Saturday evening, after having dinner with his brother, Emmett went to his bedroom to get ready for his date when Rhys came and watched him from the doorway.

'You're dressing up,' Rhys said.

'That's what you do for a date,' Emmett said. He was telling Allegra the truth about Virginia and his role in meeting her under deceptive circumstances. He just hoped she'd forgive him and give him another chance.

'But what about our movie night?'

Rhys had been building up in anxiety throughout the day, fretting about missing out on their weekly outing.

'I told you we can swap and do it tomorrow night instead,' Emmett said.

'But Sunday night is game night.' Rhys stayed home alone and had online matches with cyber buddies.

'Well, you can't have both, ' Emmett said. 'You'll have to choose. Either you have movie night tomorrow with me, or you continue game night with your friends. You can't have both.'

'But Saturday is movie night.'

Emmett internally flinched. Rhys was on the verge of a meltdown, and Emmett needed to get creative fast, or his date was going to flame and burn before he even had the chance to leave the house.

'Listen, buddy,' Emmett said. 'How about you have game night tomorrow, and afterward, we have an all-night marathon movie night at the cinema.'

It was something Rhys had been angling for ages, but while Emmett had been with Imogen, it had been an impossibility. He'd had his hands full juggling his brother and his fiancé and not making either happy, and since the breakup, Emmett had been moping and it hadn't come up.

Rhys's face lit up. 'Really, game night and all-night movies?'

'Yes.' Emmett nodded. 'Now I have to get ready, or I'm going to be late.'

He looked at his watch and felt his anxiety moving up a notch. Rhys had been following him around all night, constantly distracting him by needing things to be found, which was his strategy for managing anxiety, and now he was going to be late. He didn't even have time to do his hair and smoothed it with his hands as he walked to the car.

'Good night, Betty,' Emmett said to the babysitter as he walked through the living room.

'Have a great night,' Betty said, smiling widely. She'd never been a fan of Imogen and had been urging him to date since the breakup, even attempting to play matchmaker.

'I'll see you later tonight,' Emmett told Rhys as he got in the car.

Rhys watched him from the doorway like a lost puppy. Emmett felt relief when he was out of the driveway and on his way to pick up Allegra. He'd just make it if he hit the pedal hard. He was cruising down the freeway when he saw a police car behind him. It took him a moment to realize that it was motioning for him to pull over. He glanced at his speedometer and blanched. He was 20 miles over the speed limit.

Emmett stopped in the emergency lane and wound down his window. He waited for what felt like forever for the officer to get out of his car. Finally, the officer leaned in through the window, and Emmett handed him his license and registration.

'Is there a reason you were speeding?' the officer asked as he looked over his paperwork.

'Not really. Well, kind of,' Emmett said when the officer looked at him with disgust. 'I'm late for a date.'

'A date.' The police officer smiled.

'Yes.' Emmett smiled back. 'I'm running late, so I was speeding so I wouldn't be too late.'

'She's the kind of woman you don't want to keep waiting.'

'No.' Emmett sighed. 'She's a keeper.'

Emmett began feeling hopeful. It looked like the police officer was sympathetic to his dating drama and might let him off with a warning. He began calculating how long it would take him to get to Allegra. He estimated that if he drove at the speed limit, he would only be five minutes late, a margin that could almost be acceptable as long as he apologized profusely.

'Well, you'd better call her because we're going to be here for a while.' The police officer opened his notepad and began recording Emmett's license number.

Emmett wanted to bash his head on the steering wheel. He couldn't believe his rotten luck.

'Thanks officer,' he gritted out and lifted his mobile.

How much worse could this night get?

Chapter 7

Allegra stood by the window, her gaze fixed on the fading taillights of Emmett's departing car. Her mind whirled with emotions, leaving her feeling as unsteady as a tightrope walker on a windy day. It had been decades since she'd allowed herself to become emotionally entangled with a man, and now her senses were in turmoil. Her legs trembled beneath her, like a high-wire artist teetering on the brink of a fall from the sky. Emmett had proven himself a threat to her emotional equilibrium.

After he left, Allegra made her way upstairs, her reflection in the mirror revealing the evidence of her turbulent feelings. The makeup she had worn to their date clung to her skin, and it felt like a mask that concealed her true emotions. A shower beckoned, but there were more pressing matters at hand. She settled onto the upholstered stool before her elegant French provincial vanity table, cold cream in hand. With deliberate strokes, she smoothed the cream over her face until it resembled a delicate meringue, her eyes peeking out like distant stars in a cloudy sky. As she reached for her jewelry case, a photograph slipped out, a poignant reminder of her past—a picture of herself and Amy.

Memories flooded in of Amethyst's pain and confusion, her heartache as the police had led her away. Allegra's thoughts darkened with self-loathing; all she ever did was hurt people. The emotional entanglements she'd tried to avoid had come back to haunt her. She brushed her hair with a heavy heart, casting her gaze on the shadowy corner behind her, where an armchair sat.

'What's wrong, toots?' a voice murmured.

Startled, Allegra placed a hand over her heart. 'Oh, Henry, you scared me.'

Henry chuckled softly. 'That's what ghosts do. I've got to earn my first badge.'

'What badge?' Allegra inquired, meeting his spectral eyes in the mirror. Henry looked as she remembered, clad in the white and black-striped Gangster-style Zoot suit she'd found for him.

'It's a ghost thing,' Henry replied, removing his red fedora and twirling it playfully.

Allegra's mind drifted back to the last time she'd seen Henry, the night they'd danced together, his red fedora tilted rakishly on his head. It had been their public debut as dance partners, and she had felt like a fish out of water. The onlookers had judged her harshly, assuming she was after Henry's wealth. Little did they know that they had forged their friendship during their battles with chemotherapy, where they had supported each other through the poison meant to heal them.

As they danced, Henry had given her a reassuring smile, calming her initial apprehension. She had caught sight of the blue-rinse crowd observing them, including some of Henry's former dance partners who had harbored unrequited hopes. Yet, Henry had only ever had eyes for his late wife, Muriel, whom he mourned for two decades.

Their first dance, a Rumba, had been followed by a Cha Cha, but midway through their third set, Henry had clutched his chest in pain. Allegra knew something was terribly wrong. 'I just need a break,' he had insisted, but Allegra's dread deepened when he didn't return for their next set.

She found him in the alley behind the dance hall, his face drenched in sweat and drained of color. 'I'll get an ambulance,' Allegra had said, panic in her voice.

'No,' Henry whispered, gripping her hand. 'I want to go. It's my time.'

'No, no, it's not,' she cried, reaching for her mobile phone.

'Remember, DNR,' he whispered weakly.

Tears welled up in Allegra's eyes as she nodded, recalling that Henry had made it clear he didn't want his life unnecessarily prolonged. In the ambulance, Henry had passed away, a peaceful smile on his face, and Allegra knew he had been reunited with his beloved Muriel.

Since then, he had visited her in her dreams whenever she felt troubled, much like this morning.

'So, what are you going to do about the girl?' Henry asked, meeting her gaze in the mirror.

Allegra sighed, looking down at her hands as she removed the cold cream. 'What is there to do? I'm not her mother.'

Even mentioning Amethyst weighed heavily on her heart. 'No, you're not,' Henry agreed. 'But you're the closest thing she has.'

'It's not enough,' Allegra lamented, her hands slamming down on the vanity. 'I'm not enough. This is something I never wanted. I never wanted children or the responsibility.'

'You know better than anyone that a true family is about more than just a genetic connection,' Henry reasoned. 'It's about soul, and you felt it with her.'

'Felt what?' Allegra demanded, her voice tinged with resistance.

'You felt the spark,' Henry said. 'You felt her soul connecting with yours. The two of you are bound, whether or not you like it.'

Allegra continued to wipe off her cold cream, trying to shield herself from the impact of Henry's words, but it was too late. She remembered when Amethyst had touched her hand and the electric energy that had flowed between them.

'I don't want to,' Allegra admitted, her tone petulant. She couldn't help sounding like a child throwing a tantrum. 'I don't want this responsibility.'

'I know you don't,' Henry acknowledged. 'But you also know that if you do nothing, she will haunt you for the rest of your life. She's a part of you, and you're a part of her. You're the only one who can help her through what she's going through.'

Allegra couldn't ignore the pain in Amethyst's voice when she spoke about her Aunt Imogen. It was a pain that Allegra knew all too well. Despite all her efforts, she had never pleased her own mother, who seemed to speak an unfamiliar language. She had always felt like a misfit, as if they placed her in the wrong home. Living with her mother had been suffocating, like she was being boxed in, forced to conform to her mother's idea of a proper daughter. After her father's death, her mother sent her to boarding school at fifteen, counting the days until she turned eighteen and could escape her mother's control. She had realized that a life of privilege was akin to being a bird in a gilded cage.

Amethyst had looked to her as salvation, and she had sent her back to her aunt with little hope. She owed it to Amy's memory to do right by her daughter. Amy had been there for her when she had no one to turn to. With a heavy heart, Allegra made her decision.

She woke up from her brief nap, sprawled at the end of her bed, her face still tingling with the remnants of cold cream. She noticed the empty armchair where Henry had been sitting earlier. Allegra lay back and stared at the ceiling.

'Okay, Henry,' she said, her voice soft. 'You win. I'll see her tomorrow.'

The faint scent of Henry's aftershave lingered in the air, and for the first time in a long while, Allegra allowed herself to believe that she might be the family that Amethyst needed.

***

On Monday morning, Allegra emerged from her rejuvenating shower, her senses heightened by warm water cascading over her skin. The bathroom was filled with the invigorating aroma of her favorite lavender-scented shower gel, and the steam enveloped her like a comforting embrace.

After her cleansing ritual, she turned her attention to her wardrobe, the wooden doors creaking softly as she swung them open. The array of vintage clothing hung before her like an eclectic gallery of fashion history. As her fingers grazed the fabrics, she contemplated her choices for the day's significant visit. She had designs due later in the week for private clients who had commissioned her, but they would have to wait. This meeting required a careful balance of poise and understatement.

Her fingers glided over the selection of garments, searching for just the right ensemble. This visit was crucial, and she needed to strike the perfect tone—subdued yet dignified. Despite her penchant for vintage fashion, her calf-length pencil skirt and black jacket exuded the understated elegance she sought.

With her attire decided, she moved to her vanity, the cool, smooth surface of the tabletop welcoming her as she settled in. Her reflection in the mirror revealed the aftermath of her shower—fresh, dewy skin awaiting the embellishment of makeup. Her fingers deftly moved through the familiar motions as she applied foundation, eyeliner, and her signature bright red lipstick. Each stroke was a sensory delight, a reminder of the routine that had become an integral part of her life.

Before leaving her room, Allegra was drawn to the closet where Amethyst had once slept. Her eyes scanned the room, landing on a forgotten notebook. It was Amethyst's school notebook, nestled inconspicuously among the remnants of her stay. Allegra's fingers danced lightly over the pages until she reached the back cover, where the unexpected discovery lay—an inconspicuous gynecological report listing Allegra's full name and date of birth.

Allegra embarked on her journey to Imogen's office in Ruby, her vintage car. Taking a page from Amethyst's playbook, she had already researched her aunt online. Imogen Revett was a lawyer, and they had arranged the meeting after Allegra's breakfast call. Imogen had initially suggested an office meeting, but Allegra had opted for a neutral café, a place free from any implicit biases.

When Allegra arrived at the café, her watch showed she was three minutes late. Imogen was already seated by the window, her presence undeniable. Allegra took her seat across from her, refraining from any formalities.

'How can I help you, Mrs. Kenton?' Imogen inquired after the waitress had taken Allegra's coffee order.

'I'm Ms. Kenton,' Allegra corrected herself, her frustration bubbling beneath the surface.

'Of course,' Imogen replied with a smile that didn't quite reach her eyes.

Allegra sensed Imogen's scrutiny. She had already begun gathering information. The knowledge that Allegra had never been married seemed to be her first triumph.

'I'm here to talk about Amethyst,' Allegra stated plainly.

'I have said everything I care to on that topic,' Imogen replied, sipping her coffee.

'I know you have,' Allegra conceded, 'but I haven't.'

Imogen raised an eyebrow, prompting Allegra to continue.

'I would like to see Amethyst,' Allegra explained. 'She has some questions about her conception, and I think it would help her talk about that.'

Imogen's calm facade remained unshaken as she replied, 'I appreciate your concern for Amethyst and her well-being, but she knows everything she needs to.'

'That's not true,' Allegra retorted, the tension in her voice rising. She had come with conciliatory intentions, but Imogen's supercilious demeanor challenged her composure. 'Amethyst sought me out because she obviously doesn't know everything she needs to.'

Imogen's response was slow and patronizing. 'That was only because she thought she was adopted. Now that she knows the truth about her conception, including your role as an egg donor, she is quite satisfied.'

Allegra felt her frustration mounting, but she fought to maintain her composure. 'Still, I would like to talk to Amethyst and get to know her,' she said, her voice quivering with the effort to remain calm. 'I knew her mother. We were friends, and I want to share my memories to help her cope with her grief.'

Imogen's tone remained firm. 'Thank you for your kind offer, but Amethyst has a family. She has me to talk to about her mother. She doesn't need anyone else.'

Allegra couldn't ignore the palpable distance in Amethyst's description of her relationship with Imogen. She needed to find a way in, to be there for Amethyst without imposing herself as a parent.

'Obviously, you're not filling a need,' Allegra observed.

'I am her aunt,' Imogen responded with a sudden vehemence, rising from her seat. 'I will not justify myself any further. You are not to see her at all, and if you do, I will have you arrested.'

Allegra remained seated, unperturbed. 'Actually, I have visitation rights.'

'No, you do not,' Imogen replied, sounding less sure of herself.

Allegra produced the surrogacy agreement, passing it over to Imogen.

The document had not been her original idea. When her lawyer, her father's best friend, had reviewed the agreement, he had sensed Allegra's ambivalence.

'Are you sure you want to do this?' he had asked.

'Of course,' Allegra had nodded. 'I want to help Amy.'

That much had always been clear. Her lawyer, privy to her history, had suggested a clause that ensured Allegra would receive annual updates about any offspring resulting from her egg donation. It was a safeguard to provide peace of mind. Before the IVF treatment, Amy had been understanding of Allegra's fears. However, once she had conceived the baby, Amy had interpreted it as a sign that Allegra wanted a deeper connection with her child.

After leaving Amy's employment, Allegra received her first letter a month after the baby's birth. It had been a birth announcement, listing Amethyst Laura Revett's vital statistics—a tiny red-faced newborn captured in a photograph. Allegra had felt nothing then. She had always been ambivalent about babies, unlike those women who melted at the sight of them.

Year after year, she had received letters on Amethyst's birthday, each accompanied by a photo documenting the child's growth. Allegra had given these letters a cursory glance before stowing them away. She had been due another letter next month for Amethyst's thirteenth birthday, unaware of the significant changes in her life.

'What sort of updates?' Imogen inquired, her voice strained.

Allegra placed a stack of envelopes on the table. Imogen perused the letters and studied the photos, her expression gradually shifting from certainty to apprehension.

'I suggest you reconsider your decision,' Allegra advised calmly. 'If you don't, I will take legal action to enforce my rights.'

Imogen's fingers trembled as she gripped her handbag tight. 'I have a suggestion about how I can spend time with Amethyst without intruding on her life. Would you like to hear my proposal?'

Imogen nodded, and Allegra told her the plan.

After her meeting with Imogen, she returned to the mansion, feeling relived that she'd found a compromise that was palatable to them. As she walked up the stairs, she found a satin gold box on the porch. She lifted it carefully, reading the card. 'Can we continue our date this Saturday?' She walked into the mansion and gently opened the box.

She opened the gift box, wondering what was inside. Her previous beau's would have sent flowers or chocolate, but Emmett had sent her a set of five flower bobby hair pins. As Allegra gently caressed each pin with her finger, the ivory rose flower, coral sakura flower, mint daisy mom, coral chrysanthemum flower, and a faux pearl, she was stunned by his thoughtfulness and care.

'I think you're a keeper Emmett Dennison.' Allegra smiled sadly. She had to nip this into the bud now. Emmett was dangerous. He wasn't flirtation material. Instead, he was a man who had a serious courtship on his mind. She replied via SMS and agreed to the date on Saturday.

***

The soft chime of Allegra's phone interrupted her as she was meticulously applying her make-up. She glanced at the screen to see Emmett's name flashing with an incoming call. A devious idea crossed her mind. It was the perfect opportunity to drive a wedge in their relationship, setting the stage for her Diva Allegra persona.

With an exaggerated sigh, she dramatically accepted the call, holding the phone to her ear as if it were a heavy burden. 'Emmett,' she began feigning exasperation. 'You're late. Do you have any idea how long I've been waiting?'

Emmett's voice on the other end sounded apologetic. 'Allegra, I'm so sorry. I'm running late because I got a speeding ticket.'

'Speeding ticket?' She feigned indignation. 'Oh, Emmett, that's just great! You had one job, to be on time for our date, and you couldn't even manage that?'

'I know, I know,' Emmett replied, his voice laced with guilt. 'It was stupid of me, but the cop was hiding behind a tree, and I didn't see him until it was too late.'

Allegra couldn't help but chuckle inwardly at his explanation. 'A cop hiding behind a tree, huh? Well, Mr. Speedster, I hope you learned your lesson.'

Emmett let out a nervous laugh. 'Believe me, I have. I'll be there as soon as I can. I promise.'

Allegra leaned back in her chair, still pretending to be upset. 'Fine, but you owe me big time, Emmett. You better make this up to me.'

'I will, I promise,' he replied earnestly. 'I'll make it a night to remember, I swear.'

'Good,' Allegra said. 'Just hurry. I'll be here waiting.'

She had to ensure that Emmett chose to walk away, and the only way to achieve that was to unleash Diva Allegra. Allegra sat down on the edge of the bed, deep in thought. Her original plan had been to keep Emmett waiting for at least half an hour before their date, and that's why she hadn't even begun getting dressed. Now, he had thrown a wrench into her plans.

Her fingers glided over the array of garments in her wardrobe as she contemplated her options. Finally, she settled on her Charleston cream dress with intricate bone Art Deco embroidery, featuring two layers of beaded fringe along the hemline. Complementing the dress, she chose a cream headband adorned with a pristine white feather and donned a pair of elegant white satin gloves. Emmett had shown discomfort in the past when she dressed to stand out, and Diva Allegra thrived on attention. As she meticulously applied her makeup, she kept a vigilant eye on the clock, realizing she needed to get downstairs and make it appear as though she had been waiting for him.

Twenty minutes later, she gracefully descended the stairs, and just as she reached the bottom, Emmett's car headlights illuminated the living room. She rushed to open the door for him before he reached it himself.

'I'm sorry I'm late,' he apologized as he hurried toward her. 'Wow, you look amazing,' he added, stopping in his tracks to admire her.

'Thanks,' Allegra replied with a coy smile. 'I had plenty of time to get ready.'

'Sorry, it was just bad luck,' Emmett explained, running a hand through his hair.

Allegra paused for effect, letting feigned displeasure hang in the air. He looked so vulnerable and endearing that she momentarily wanted to drop the Diva act and simply enjoy his company. 'Okay,' she relented and walked toward the passenger seat.

Emmett held the car door open for her, but Allegra remained silent during the drive to the restaurant, rebuffing his attempts at small talk. She cranked up the music, drowning out his words in a wall of sound.

Upon their arrival at the restaurant, she waited for him to open the car door, signaling her reluctance. The two of them entered the establishment in silence, with Allegra intentionally keeping her distance. Upon reaching the concierge, Emmett inquired about his reservation, only to be told there was no such booking.

'I booked this two days ago,' Emmett insisted, forcing a strained smile in Allegra's direction. 'Could we have a table?'

'Sorry, sir,' the concierge replied. 'We're fully booked. The only available option is to wait until our first booking clears, which will be in an hour.'

Allegra stepped back, distancing herself as Emmett continued to argue with the concierge. She couldn't help but feel a pang of sympathy for him. He had clearly put in a lot of effort to impress her with this elegant restaurant choice, yet something had gone awry. If she wanted to salvage the date, she would suggest going elsewhere, smoothing over his embarrassment and awkwardness. However, her ulterior motive restrained her until Emmett had concluded his conversation with the concierge.

'I'm sorry about this,' Emmett said, looking apologetic. 'I made a reservation.'

'Of course,' Allegra replied, her tone empathetic. 'Maybe we should just call it a night. It seems like this isn't working out.'

Emmett scrutinized her face, and she could sense the hurt he was trying to conceal.

'I'll drive you home,' he offered.

'No,' Allegra insisted, stepping back further. 'I think it's best if I catch a taxi.'

Emmett's lips tightened as he suppressed his frustration. 'I drove you here, and I will drive you back,' he said, not meeting her gaze as he extended a hand, gesturing toward the restaurant entrance.

Allegra nodded, joining him by his side. Her plan had succeeded all too well, as if the universe had conspired to grant her wish. Emmett wouldn't have the courage to ask her out again. She couldn't understand why that made her feel a twinge of sadness. She should have been relieved to be rid of the complication he represented.

Chapter 8

They emerged from the restaurant and stood under the dimly lit awning, waiting. The evening air was filled with the distant traffic sounds and the occasional murmur of conversation from passersby. Soft lights from nearby storefronts cast a warm glow on the cobblestone pavement.

Minutes slipped by, and the valet, tasked with retrieving Emmett's car, remained conspicuously absent. The night was quiet except for the soft rustling of leaves in the nearby trees. Suddenly, the serenity was shattered by the persistent beeping of a car alarm and the sound of raised voices.

Emmett turned to Allegra, his expression a mix of frustration and concern. 'Stay here,' he instructed, his voice firm but tinged with worry, and he began striding toward the car park.

He heard the clack of her high heels as she followed. That woman was determined to throw herself in the path of danger. He slowed and took her arm, wanting to make sure he was near her so he could protect her from danger.

As they turned a corner, Emmett saw it was his car that was beeping. Standing beside it was a valet and a young man shouting and banging his head with his fists.

'Stay right there while I call the police,' the valet was saying, a mobile against his ear.

Rhys continued to move erratically, disoriented and overwhelmed. Emmett reached his side. 'Rhys, I'm here. It's okay. I'm here.'

'I found him trying to get in the car,' the valet said. 'When I grabbed him, he went mental and started shouting.'

'He doesn't like to be touched,' Emmett said. 'Rhys, I'm here. It's okay. I'm here.'

Rhys briefly glanced up at Emmett, his eyes reflecting confusion, before lowering his gaze to the ground.

Emmett spoke gently, his voice soothing, 'I'm going to put my hand on your neck, okay, buddy.'

Rhys didn't react as Emmett gently reached out his hand. When Emmett put his hand on his neck, Rhys dropped his hands from his head and stood still. The two brothers stood in silence, and calm descended.

'I think we're okay,' Allegra told the valet. 'This is for your trouble.' She handed him a large tip. With one last look, the valet walked away.

'Are you okay?' Emmett asked. Rhys nodded, and Emmett dropped his hand and stepped away. 'How did you get here?'

'I told Betty I was going to play video games in my room and snuck out past her,' Rhys said.

'I'd better call Betty and tell her I've got you.' Emmett picked up his phone and called.

Rhys looked over at Allegra. He frowned as he looked her up and down. 'Why are you dressed like you're going to a costume party?' he asked.

'Rhys,' Emmett burst out, his voice tight with frustration after he finished on the phone.

'It's okay,' Allegra said. 'I dress like this because I like old-fashioned clothing. This is called a flapper dress, and it's from the Roaring Twenties, which is the 1920s.'

Rhys tilted his head. 'You look very interesting.'

'Thank you,' Allegra smiled.

'Rhys, this is my date, Allegra,' Emmett introduced them.

'Nice to meet you,' Allegra said, not offering her hand.

She impressed Emmett. Most people didn't listen to cues and still automatically offered to shake hands.

'Get in the back seat and put on your seat belt. I'll just be a moment.' Emmett walked over to Allegra. 'I'm so sorry about my brother. He has autism and struggles in social situations. He must have followed me because he was upset about our date.'

'I'm just glad that he's okay,' Allegra said.

'Yes.' Emmett rubbed his hand over his face. 'He's fine now. Come on, we'll give you a ride home.'

Allegra hesitated.

'Of course, I can also call you a taxi.' What was he thinking? Of course, she wanted nothing to do with him.

'No, I want you to drive me. I don't want to upset Rhys.' She stopped forward and put her hand on his arm. He looked down at her up-turned face. She was looking at him with such compassion. Guilt squeezed his gut.

'Listen, I don't know if I'll get the chance to tell you this, so here goes. I met you under deceptive circumstances. I was helping my friend Virginia, who wanted to overturn her uncle's will. That's why I wanted to see you tonight, to tell you.'

'Oh,' her mouth formed a perfect moue of surprise.

'Soon after meeting you, I realized she was lying about the circumstances of the inheritance and told her I wouldn't have anything to do with her. You don't have to feel compelled to continue this disaster of a date. I'm a liar, and you owe me nothing.'

He turned around and sat in the car, avoiding looking at her as he started the car.

The passenger door opened, and Allegra sat in the passenger seat. 'Do you mind giving me a lift?'

Emmett froze, his key in the ignition. 'Sure, we'll be happy to give you a lift. Rhys?'

Rhys didn't speak from the backseat, so Emmett started the car.

'I'm sorry,' Rhys burst out when Emmett began driving.

'I know, buddy.' Emmett looked at Rhys in the rearview mirror. 'You shouldn't have left home.'

'No, I'm sorry about the restaurant,' Rhys said.

Emmet stilled. 'Did you cancel my reservation?' he asked.

Rhys nodded.

'I am furious with you,' Emmett said, his hands tight on the steering wheel. 'We will talk about the consequences of your behavior when we get home.'

Rhys was silent for a few minutes. 'Is Allegra your girlfriend?' he asked, his head popping up between them.

'Rhys, manners please,' Emmett said. 'And sit back and put on your seatbelt.'

Rhys complied. 'So, is she your girlfriend?' Rhys asked again.

'No, we just went on a date, but now I'm taking Allegra home.'

'I thought you said that a date was having dinner together.'

'Well, we couldn't do that,' Emmett said, his voice showing the strain of containing his frustration.

'But I'm hungry. Maybe we can all have a date together,' Rhys said.

'It doesn't work like that,' Emmett said.

'Actually, that's a great idea,' Allegra said, turning to look at Rhys. 'What would you like to eat?'

'It's okay. I don't want to make you more uncomfortable,' Emmett said.

'I'm hungry too, and I think it would be nice if we all had dinner together. Do you like Italian food?' Allegra asked.

'I love pizza,' Rhys said.

'Just turn left here,' Allegra directed Emmett. 'I know a good Italian restaurant.'

After they'd placed their orders, Rhys wandered over to the fish tank in the restaurant's foyer, mesmerized by the colorful fish gliding through the water.

Emmett sighed, leaning closer to Allegra. 'I'm sorry about tonight,' he said. 'He gets threatened by a change in routine and was scared he'd have to share me. My last relationship didn't end well. My fiancé wasn't willing to be an instant mother to a then 13-year-old and broke it off.'

'What happened to your parents?' Allegra asked.

'My father was never much of a family man, and when Mom was diagnosed with early on-set dementia and had to go into a home, he divorced her and re-married three months ago. He wanted to put Rhys into an institution, but I couldn't let that happen. He's my brother.'

Allegra took hold of his hand.

'Anyway, you can see how this doesn't make me a bachelor of the year,' Emmett pulled away and forced a smile.

Allegra's expression turned apologetic. 'I'm sorry about tonight too,' she admitted, her guilt evident. 'I was purposely difficult in the beginning because I wanted to put you off.'

Emmett was taken aback. 'Why?' he asked, genuinely curious.

With a sigh, Allegra revealed her vulnerability. 'Because I was scared,' she confessed. 'I've just recovered from breast cancer, and everything in my life has changed. I feel like a different person, and I don't even know who that person is.'

Emmett's eyes softened, and he reached across the table and gently held her hand. 'Well, if it matters at all, I like the person you are now.'

Allegra's lips curled into a warm smile, and their eyes locked in an unspoken connection.

Their food arrived, filling the air with delicious aromas, and Emmett called Rhys back to the table.

'Rhys, what are your favorite things to do?' Allegra asked as she twirled her spaghetti bolognese.

'Playing video games and chess.' Rhys speared his penne, which glistened from the sauteed butter they had served at his request.

'Would you like to ask Allegra something now, buddy?' Emmett encouraged after there was a lull in the conversation.

Rhys looked at him inquisitively. 'Oh, of course. What are your favorite things to do?' he asked Allegra.

'I love dancing and vintage fashion.' Allegra smiled, her blue eyes sparkling.

His heart melted as Emmett watched her patiently coax Rhys into a conversation. He couldn't believe that the date that had begun as a disaster was turning into the best night of his life. And that Allegra had so eagerly forgiven him for lying to her. He felt a moment of disquiet. She had accepted his apology so quickly, that his lawyer's mind prodded him. He shook off his suspicion. He just needed to take this for what it was.

'So what are we going to do now?' Rhys asked. 'We have twenty minutes until the movie.'

'Rhys, I told you, we're not having a movie night tonight.'

'But we had pizza,' Rhys said. 'Movie night is always after pizza.'

Emmett started arguing with him.

'A movie sounds great,' Allegra said. 'What are we going to watch?'

Allegra and Rhys rose from their seats in anticipation of the movie, but Emmett remained seated, momentarily lost in thought.

'Come on, we're going to be late,' Allegra urged, her voice carrying a hint of excitement.

They purchased their tickets at the cinema and entered the darkened theater just as the advanced screenings started. The dimmed lights, the rustling of fellow moviegoers, and the scent of buttered popcorn created a sensory tapestry that enveloped them.

Rhys, clutching a soft drink and a bag of popcorn, was instantly captivated by the on-screen action, his eyes fixed on the unfolding story.

Emmett leaned closer to Allegra and whispered, 'I'm sorry about this.'

Her eyes glued to the screen, Allegra whispered, 'Nothing to be sorry about. I've been wanting to watch this movie for weeks and haven't had a chance to.'

Allegra's face lit up with joy and wonder as the film's story unfolded before their eyes. Her occasional gasps, laughter, and the sparkle in her eyes revealed her joy. Emmett couldn't help but watch her, and in that moment, her happiness and contentment became the most beautiful scenes in the theater.

After the movie, Rhys walked ahead of them.

'Thank you for being so good with him,' Emmett said. 'Not many people have patience for his idiosyncrasies.'

'I had a good time,' Allegra said.

'I truly doubt that,' Emmett said.

'No, I really did,' Allegra said. 'I was actually hoping that I wouldn't.'

'Why?' Emmett asked.

'I'm not in a place in my life right now where I want to date. There are a lot of complications, and I feel like I need some time and space to work through those with no distractions.'

'That sounds like a line that women say when trying to shake someone off,' Emmett said.

'It does, doesn't it?' Allegra said.

'I'm sorry,' Emmett stopped her. 'I'm being arrogant and making all this about me when I know better than most about complicated. That's why I was pushing so hard to make this into something. I feel like the complications are becoming my life.'

'I know,' Allegra said. 'I'm kind of scared of that. Maybe you and I can do something I've never done with another man before.'

'What?' Emmett asked.

'Take it slow and let things develop more naturally.'

'Yes, but how do I know I won't be stuck in the friend's zone,' Emmett said.

'I don't know,' Allegra said. 'But you're the first guy I wanted to try with.'

Emmett hesitated. He met her eyes, and they looked at each other. Something passed between them, something he hadn't felt before.

'You're the first man I want to get to know properly. I want you to know the real me and not the persona I put on display.'

She gestured to her vintage outfit, and he realized that dressing like a vintage doll was a way of expressing her love of vintage fashion, but it was also a costume that she could don and play a role in.

'Okay,' Emmett said. 'Let's take it slow.'

He had to trust that she wanted them to have more than sex, and with the complications in his life, he needed to know that it was for real before opening himself up again.

Emmett drove her home. 'Wait in the car,' he told Rhys before he got out and walked around to open the car door for Allegra.

'Are you going to marry Emmett?' he heard Rhys ask through the open window.

'No,' Allegra said. 'I thought I'd date him first. Is that okay with you?'

'Do you like him?' Rhys asked.

Allegra took a deep breath. 'Yes,' Allegra said. 'Yes, I do.'

Emmett felt a sweep of containment. It was enough for now.

'Good. His last girlfriend didn't like him. She was always bossing him around. I think it's good that you date him.' Emmet winced - out of the mouths of babes. Sometimes they got to the heart of the matter in the most direct way. He didn't want to think about Imogen now.

Emmett opened her door, and she stepped out, holding his hand.

'Thank you for a wonderful night,' Emmett said as he walked her to the front door.

'Thank you,' Allegra said.

They hesitated for a moment. He could feel Rhys' stare from the car. She leaned forward and kissed Emmett on the cheek. He smiled.

The car door opened, and Rhys poked his head out.

'I told you to stay in the car,' Emmett said.

'I am.'

'Sorry,' Emmett said. 'He can't last long.'

'That's okay. I should probably get inside.'

'I'll call you,' Emmett said.

'Please,' Allegra whispered, the word a plea and promise in one.

He glanced at Rhys in the car, his face pressed against the glass window. He so desperately wanted to kiss her; instead, he squeezed her hand and left.

Chapter 9

As Allegra watched Emmett's car pull away, a mixture of emotions swirled within her. Her lips tingled with the phantom sensation of a kiss she wished they had shared. Regret crept over her, like a shadow obscuring the moonlight, as she replayed their date in her mind.

She remembered how, at the beginning of the evening, she had tried to sabotage it, testing Emmett's patience. The memory of her feigned anger and resistance to his charm weighed on her. She had been so afraid, afraid of the vulnerability that came with dating again after recovering from breast cancer, afraid of being seen for who she truly was.

But now, as she stood alone on the sidewalk, the nervous excitement coursing through her veins, she realized something important. Despite her attempts to push Emmett away, he had been patient, understanding, and kind. His willingness to see past her defensive facade had touched her in a way she hadn't expected.

With each passing moment, she felt more alive than she had in a long time. The prospect of a new beginning, a fresh chapter in her life, stirred something deep within her. It was as if the clouds of uncertainty were parting, revealing a glimmer of sunshine.

She couldn't deny the attraction she felt for Emmett, nor the genuine connection they had shared during their date. It was a chance at happiness she had almost denied herself.

Allegra knew that embracing this new path wouldn't be without its challenges and uncertainties, but she also knew that sometimes, taking a leap of faith was the only way to find what had been missing in her life. With a hopeful smile, she turned away from the receding taillights and walked toward her future, ready to explore the possibilities that lay ahead. Tomorrow, she would take another step in opening up her heart.

***

Allegra felt strangely nervous as she walked up to the school gates. She'd walked through these gates so many times before as a young woman, and while sometimes she'd felt trepidation, it was nothing compared to this low-level nervousness she was feeling.

Mark was beside her. 'All good?' he asked. 'You seem subdued.'

'No, I'm fine,' Allegra said. 'Just have things on my mind.'

He nodded without pushing. She and Mark had been an item the year before, and even though they had broken up, Mark was still perceptive. They had settled into a comfortable routine, as if their romance had happened in another lifetime. She was grateful that she had Mark as a stabilizing influence as she entered the school. When she'd told him about delivering lessons to high school students, he'd seen it as a promotional dream and jumped at the chance. They had discussed starting their own dance studio and offering Le Bop lessons, and this was their trial run.

An office staff member led them into the performing arts studio, and Mark started setting up the music track while Allegra looked around. It had been upgraded since she was in school and looked completely different. There was a mirror that folded out of the way. The school had dance lessons, but Mrs. Philips had been excited at the thought of the Lebop dance and the opportunity to incorporate an exhibition performance at the next school graduation ceremony.

She was nervous about seeing Amethyst again. There had been so much confusion and pain in her face the last time they saw each other when the police led her away. Allegra honestly didn't know if she was doing the right thing. Was she stirring up more memories for Amethyst rather than letting time heal? But then again, she knew better than anyone that a child never truly healed after losing a parent. She'd been ten years old when her father passed away, and she still felt anguish as she marked milestones in her life and didn't have the supportive hand of her beloved father to hold on to.

She and Mark began practicing, and Allegra got lost in the zone, when she saw her students entering the performing arts. She saw Amethyst over her shoulder, and her face held such joy and curiosity that Allegra was wrenched back to earth. As the teacher supervising their session introduced her and Mark, Allegra was aware of Amethyst, like she was a hot spot in her vision. The girl's eyes did not move away from Allegra.

Allegra and Mark began their dancing demonstration, and Amethyst followed the steps, her brow creased in concentration. Mark and Allegra split up, providing one-on-one corrections to the girls. Mark walked past when Amethyst and Allegra stood side by side and did a double-take.

'Are the two of you sisters?' he asked.

Amethyst's face lit up.

'Something like that,' Allegra said.

'Why didn't you tell him the truth?' Amethyst asked when Mark had moved away.

'It's a bit personal,' Allegra said.

'But isn't he your boyfriend?' Amethyst asked. 'I saw the two of you kissing after the Primo awards. Why didn't you tell him?'

'We're not seeing each other anymore.'

'What happened? Why did you break up? Is it because of me?' Amethyst asked, sounding panicked.

'Slow down.' Allegra held up her hands. 'Firstly, nothing happened. Sometimes people just realize they're not compatible anymore. Secondly, it wasn't a breakup so much as a drift away, and no, it has nothing to do with you. We're still friends. As you can see.'

Mark gestured to Allegra. As Allegra went to stand beside him to demonstrate the next move, she was relieved to have an excuse to move away from Amethyst's probing questions. While she'd come here to give Amethyst an opportunity to get to know her, she hadn't realized how confronting it would be.

After the dance lesson, all the girls drifted out except Amethyst, who waited by the radio. 'It's lunchtime now,' she said. 'I was wondering if you had time to stay and eat with me.' Amethyst held up her lunchbox. 'I packed an extra sandwich.'

'I'm not sure,' Allegra said, looking over at Mark.

'You can go. I'll pack these up and bring them over tonight,' Mark said, gesturing toward the music box. They were doing their dance rehearsal at Allegra's house.

'All right.' Allegra nodded.

'I want to show you something,' Amethyst said shyly.

Allegra followed her down the sports grounds and to a copse of trees.

'Not many students come here.' Amethyst held up a branch. 'That's why I like it.' She walked to a log under a tree and sat down.

Allegra sat beside her and looked around. While she could still see the sports ground through holes in the branches, to all intents and purposes, they were camouflaged from the other students playing various sports.

'Hope you like PBJ's.' Amethyst handed her a sandwich from her lunchbox and a juice box.

'Love them.' Amethyst took a bite.

They ate in silence for a moment.

'There's something I've wanted to ask,' Amethyst said.

'Go ahead.' Allegra sipped from the juice box.

'How come you don't have any children?'

'You don't pull any punches,' Allegra said, feeling put on the spot. Seeing Amethyst's face, she knew she didn't want to lie to her. 'Some women want to have children, and some women, like me, don't.'

'So you don't want to have children, ever?' Amethyst asked, her voice full of disbelief.

Allegra shook her head.

A group of students entered the woods. After looking at them curiously, they moved away a few meters and sat down, murmuring among themselves as they ate lunch.

'Are you sure?' Amethyst asked, lowering her voice. 'Maybe you just haven't spent enough time around kids and don't know you want children.'

She'd heard that statement too many times, and it got her blood boiling. Her not wanting children had been a fact ever since she could remember. Whenever adults in her life had told her she'd change her mind when she got older, she'd always thought to herself, *no, I won't.* And she never had. If anything, as she got older, it just reconfirmed for her she wasn't maternal.

She took a breath and calmed herself before replying to Amethyst. 'Some of us don't find children the most interesting thing in the world and have other things to do. Besides which, I hate that old cliche that all women should want to have children.'

'Sorry,' Amethyst said. 'It's just something my Mom said.'

'I know. Your mother was always baby crazy. She could never understand someone that wasn't.'

Amy was a woman for whom the term Earth Mother was invented. All who knew her had experienced her maternal nature as she took care of them, always having food, a shoulder to cry on, and sage advice.

'Tell me more,' Amethyst asked, her eyes wide with curiosity.

'Well, she used to come over when I was little, and she loved playing with me. I remember her mom said that Amy never wanted to play with dolls. Instead, she always looked for babies that she could play with.'

Amy used to dress Allegra in a frilly little dress that she'd make herself, and it was her influence that had inspired Allegra's love of fashion.

'So you knew my Mom since you were little?'

'I don't remember a time when I didn't know your Mom. Our parents were friends for a very long time.'

Their fathers were college roommates and had remained best friends after graduating. They had always joked that an administrator with a sense of humor must have allocated them to the same room since her father's surname was Wren and Amy's father's was Finch. After Allegra's father passed away, their mothers had not gotten along, but Amy had been ten years older and had stepped in as a sibling and babysitter, so they had remained close.

'How come we never met?' Amethyst asked.

'Things changed,' Allegra tried to evade. 'We weren't as close.'

'But why?'

It embarrassed Allegra to tell her the truth. She hated remembering the naive idiot she had been and the way she'd believed Cole. She also didn't want to tell Amethyst that her mother had feared that Allegra would develop an attachment for her as a baby and had distanced herself from her.

'We drifted apart. Your mother had you, and I was focusing on my career, and we fell out of touch.'

Amethyst frowned as she processed this. Allegra prayed inside that she would buy into her white lie.

'Why did Aunt Imogen let you come here and see me? I heard her saying that she would hire a lawyer and make sure we never saw each other, then suddenly she changed her mind.'

Allegra should have felt relief that Amethyst had moved onto another topic, but this one was just as sticky as the previous one. Allegra didn't want to say anything negative about Imogen, but she also had to tell Amethyst the truth.

'Well, your Aunt Imogen didn't understand the situation. She thought I wanted to take you away.'

'But don't you?' Amethyst looked at her with hopeful eyes again. 'Don't you want to be my mother?'

Allegra felt the familiar choking sensation as she felt the weight of responsibility toward Amethyst. 'I'm not fit to be anyone's mother,' Allegra said.

Amethyst recoiled, and Allegra felt guilty. She'd forgotten that Amethyst was a child and had to be spoken to as one.

'I want to be your friend. Someone that you can talk to,' Allegra said gently. She lifted her hand, holding it behind Amethyst's back. She wanted to place it gently on her and comfort her, but somehow, it felt too fraught to engage in physical contact. Their conversation was already an emotional minefield. If she tried to comfort her, Amethyst would take that as a sign of maternal affection. Allegra returned her hand to her side.

'Like the way you and my mother were. Sort of like sisters.' Amethyst smiled.

'Something like that,' Allegra said.

Amethyst hesitated, her face troubled as if trying to decide whether to say something. 'But my aunt says I shouldn't trust you,' she said slowly.

Allegra took a deep breath, holding back what she truly wanted to say about Imogen. 'Your Aunt is doing what every aunt should do,' she said instead. 'She's looking out for you. She wants only the best for you, but we can be friends. You already have a mother. The best mother you could ever ask for.' Allegra went to her handbag and got out a photo. It was of Amethyst and Amy at a park. Amethyst was six years old with a gap-toothed smile as her front teeth had fallen out. They were beaming as they each held a cone, their cheeks flushed from the sun. 'This is your Mom, and no one can ever take her place. Most importantly, nobody should try.'

'How did you get this photo?' Amethyst asked, taking it gently by the edges as she caressed her mother's face with a finger.

'Your Mom sent it to me. She wanted me to see that you were well taken care of.'

Amethyst peered into her handbag and saw the other photos in a packet. 'Why are they in envelopes?'

'I didn't look at them until you came to my door.'

'Why? Didn't you want to know how I was doing?' Amethyst asked.

'I didn't need to,' Allegra lied. 'I knew you were loved and taken care of because I knew Amy was the best mother in the world. Some women are made to be mothers, and she was one of them.'

Amethyst didn't need to know that she hadn't looked at the photos because she had been worried that Amy was right, and if she saw the child who looked like her, she would feel a connection that she had no right to feel.

They heard the chiming of the school bell on the breeze. The students on the sports ground began drifting away.

'Lunchtime is over,' Amethyst said, her voice glum.

'That's okay. We'll see each other again next week.' Allegra risked placing her hand on Amethyst's. 'I'll stay for lunch again.'

Amethyst smiled, her eyes brightening as she held onto Allegra's hand.

'We'd better clean this up,' Allegra said, pulling her hand away so she could pick up her empty juice box. As they walked back to the front gate, Amethyst walked beside her with a bounce in her footsteps.

'Thanks for the sandwich,' Allegra said. 'I'll bring lunch next time.'

Amethyst smiled and hesitated before quickly stepping forward and hugging Allegra. Before Allegra had the chance to decide whether to curve her arms around her, Amethyst let go and ran to class. As Allegra walked toward her car, she wondered whether feeling this mingling of panic and fear was normal. She wanted to get in her car, drive away from the school, and never return.

As Allegra walked back to her car, her mind was still buzzing from her lunchtime encounter with Amethyst. She couldn't help but feel a mixture of emotions—joy at having reconnected with the girl but also a gnawing sense of unease about the complexities of their relationship.

As she reached her car, she spotted Emmett waiting for her by the entrance to the school. His warm smile and the way his eyes lit up when he saw her sent a flutter through her chest. She knew he had been honest with her about his past, about Rhys, and it made her feel guilty for not sharing her own secrets.

Chapter 10

Emmett was waiting for Rhys at his school when he saw Allegra. As she walked, it seemed as if the crowd was parting for her. She looked like she'd stepped out of a 1950s movie in her black and white diagonally striped full-skirted dress, and the other parents waiting for their children watched her pass.

'Allegra,' he called her name. She looked at him in shock. 'This is a surprise. What are you doing here?' he asked.

'Emmett.' She turned toward him and hitched her handbag higher on her shoulder. 'I'm visiting Mrs Phillips.'

'You are.' He lifted his eyebrow, surprised that she knew the Principal. 'How do you two know each other?'

'I'm a former student,' Allegra said.

Emmett was confused. Most of the students were children of celebrities or trust fund babies, although a small percentage of students were local to the area and on scholarship.

'And you. Is this Rhys' school?' Allegra asked.

Emmett nodded. 'His father is an alum, and Rhys' paternal grandparents are paying the school fees.'

'How is Joleen doing?' Emmett asked, wanting to break the awkward silence that had descended. He'd tried calling her for a follow-up date, but she'd told him she had to take a rain check because Joleen ended up in hospital with broken ribs.

'She's much better, thank you,' Allegra sighed.

'I'm glad to hear it,' Emmett said. He put his hands in his pocket and rocked back on his feet as he worked up the courage to ask her. 'Is your schedule clear now?' He held his breath as he waited for an answer.

'It sure is.' Allegra smiled flirtatiously.

Emmett felt happiness fill him. She was definitely interested. 'Can I cash in that rain check?' he asked.

'Of course.' Allegra got her phone out.

They agreed to a date Saturday night because she had a dance competition on Friday.

'I'll see you then,' Allegra said, giving him a quick peck on the cheek.

Emmett held himself in check as he breathed in her scent. She took his breath away. He couldn't wait for their date.

After she'd disappeared in the crowd, he glanced at his watch. 'Shit,' he groaned and rushed to the performing arts rooms that were being transformed into a chess tournament. When he arrived, the tournament had begun, and there was hushed conversation, the clicking sounds of chess clocks being hit and wooden chess pieces clacking as they were moved. He looked for Rhys, who was easy to spot. He was the only person standing, and an official was gesturing toward a chair.

'You will have to forfeit the championship if you do not begin the match,' Emmett overheard the official saying when he was close enough.

'I'm here,' Emmett said, out of breath when he reached his brother.

Rhys sat down. The official looked perturbed. Emmett smiled and whispered an apology. The official stepped back with a nod.

Rhys hit the button on the chess clock. After deliberating for 3 seconds, he made his first move. Emmett breathed out. His mother attended every single chess tournament with Rhys, and once she became too ill to manage it, Emmett took over. Rhys had a routine, and he struggled with any deviation, and if Emmett hadn't arrived, he could have quite possibly forfeited the tournament, leading to a meltdown of epic proportions.

Emmett watched the tournament and was on hand to congratulate his brother when he won again. 'You did it. You're going to the next round.'

Rhys nodded but didn't smile.

After the ceremony awarding the winners, he and Emmett stepped out. 'I thought we could go to the *Barney's Burgers* to celebrate,' Emmett said, naming Rhys' favorite burger joint.

'Why were you late?' Rhys asked abruptly.

'I got held up,' Emmett said as he reversed. He glanced over and saw Rhys' face. 'I saw Allegra, the woman I had a date with, at your school. We were arranging another date.'

'When?' Rhys demanded.

'Actually, it's on Saturday night.' Emmett turned on his blinkers and waited for the lights.

'But Saturday night is movie night,' Rhys said.

Usually, they went to the movies together every Saturday night and had burgers beforehand.

'I know,' Emmett said. 'But that's why we're going to have a burger now, and Betty will come and be with you on Saturday night. That's okay, isn't it?'

'I don't like you dating,' Rhys said.

Emmett sighed, knowing that from Rhys' point of view, Emmett's dating was all about a disruption of the status quo.

'I know, buddy,' Emmett said as he parked the car. 'But this woman, well, she's something special.'

'Do you love her?' Rhys asked.

'No, I don't love her.' Emmett turned off the car and took out the keys. 'It's too early for that, but I really, really like her, and it would mean a lot to me if you supported me so I could see her.' He turned in his seat and waited for Rhys' response.

Rhys nodded and opened the car door. Emmett followed slowly. He had a feeling this would be a conversation that would continue.

***

He pulled into Allegra's driveway and sighed as he looked at his dashboard clock. He was ten minutes early. Emmet realized he should have driven around the block, but he'd been so determined to set a different tone to this date that he'd left much earlier than he needed to. He walked to the door and rang the doorbell. There was silence for a few minutes, and then the sound of high heels.

The front door opened, and Allegra looked at him with surprise. 'You're early,' she wailed.

'Sorry,' Emmett said. 'I could go and come back.'

Allegra bit her lip before shaking her head. 'It doesn't matter. You might as well find out what you've gotten yourself into. Wow, they're beautiful,' she said, notching the flowers in his arms.

He'd made a special order and had the florist create a vintage flower arrangement using an old tin as a vase.

She gave him a quick peck on the cheek and took the flowers out of his arms. 'Thank you.'

He followed her to the kitchen, carrying a bottle of red wine, admiring how the red and black polka dot dress curved around her waist.

'As you can see, I haven't gotten very far.' Allegra waved her hand at the messy bench top.

'What are you making?' Emmett asked, removing his jacket and placing it on a kitchen chair.

Allegra handed him a magazine cut out. 'Joleen gave it to me. She said that even someone with my limited culinary ability should be able to do it, but she was wrong. So wrong.'

'Spicy Beef and Broccoli Noodle Bowl. Sounds lovely.' Emmett rolled up his sleeves. 'Where's your chopping board?'

After Allegra handed him the chopping board and he'd found the sharpest knife in her knife block, he began trimming the meat. Allegra removed her centerpiece and placed the flowers in the middle of the kitchen table.

'You seem to know your way around a knife block,' she said as she opened the wine.

'One perk of being a bachelor. I had to learn to cook or live off two-minute noodles.' He'd finished trimming the fat and wiped his hands on a tea towel. Allegra handed him a glass, and he took a sip. 'Where's your frying pan?'

After Allegra had found the pan, he poured oil and began searing the beef.

'Well, living on my own did nothing to develop my cooking skills.' Allegra took a sip of her wine.

'I'm not surprised,' Emmett said. 'A beautiful woman like you wouldn't much need to cook. You were probably being wined and dined every night of the week.'

Allegra nodded wryly. 'I guess so. Although learning to cook would have probably served me better.'

'There's no time like the present,' Emmett beckoned her over.

Allegra came, and he moved so she stood in front of him. 'Hold the handle like this and move the strips around.' As he held the handle with her, he found it hard to concentrate with her naked shoulders exposed in the halter-neck dress.

'Aren't they ready?' Allegra asked, looking at him over her shoulder.

'Yes, yes, they are,' Emmett said, quickly stepping away. 'Let's take them out to drain here.'

As he took her through the recipe step by step, bolstered by sips of wine, they laughed and relaxed in each other's company.

'There, you have now added a new recipe to your repertoire,' Emmett said as they sat down to eat.

'To many more culinary experiments,' Allegra said, raising her glass in a toast.

As their glasses clinked, their eyes caught in the moment, and a charged silence filled them.

'I think we should try this now.' Allegra picked up her chopsticks and expertly fished out a beef strip and noodles. 'Yum,' she said after she swallowed.

Emmett followed and nodded in agreement.

'So Rhys was all right with our date tonight?' Allegra asked.

'He's not very comfortable with changes to routine. It's part of his condition, but now that he knows you, he approves.' Emmett took another sip of wine. That was an understatement of the century. Rhys thrived on routine, and any variation set him into a meltdown.

'Did he get along with your fiancé?' Allegra held her glass between her palms and watched him as she waited for an answer.

'No, she wasn't very keen on being an instant parent, and the two didn't get along.' Emmett stifled a smile as he remembered Rhys' revenge when his fiancé high-jacked one of their get-togethers. Rhys took her keys from her purse and flushed them down the toilet. Emmett had to fish them out and get the entire set re-cut because Imogen had refused to use the keys afterward. 'There's not many women who have taken a shine to Rhys, but you seem to have taken it in your stride.' He'd had a few dates since breaking up with Imogen and while some of his dates had professed that they were all right with Rhys, when confronted with the reality of his idiosyncrasies, they were very short on patience.

'I've experienced my very own complication.' Allegra looked at the table as she spoke, as if she feared his reaction. 'I was an egg donor when I was 20 years old. The little girl born from my donation made contact recently and wants us to have a relationship.'

'You sound ambivalent about having a relationship with her,' Emmett said, picking up on the tension in her voice.

'I understand why she would want to have a relationship, considering our genetic link. I just don't know if it's a good idea. There are some women who are maternal, and there are women like me.' She took a sip of wine and tilted her head. 'You see, I never wanted to have children.'

She watched as if waiting for a reaction to her statement. 'I think it's good that you know your mind,' he said.

'Not everyone agrees. I've been called selfish for not wanting to have children.' She smiled sadly.

'I think it's the opposite of selfish. There are lots of people who shouldn't have been parents but lack the self-awareness to acknowledge it.' Emmett thought of his father but pushed his bitterness away. He didn't want memories of his father to taint his date. 'It's very noble that you wanted to help someone else conceive.'

'Altruism did not motivate me. There was a payment involved.'

She said it as if she were daring him to think the worst of her. 'I don't believe you just did it for the money,' Emmett said slowly.

'Why?' Allegra asked. 'You just met me. How can you know I wasn't motivated by money?'

Emmett didn't get to where he was without learning to read people. Allegra was sitting up straight and holding her breath as she maintained eye contact. She was trying to sell him an image of herself as a cold, heartless woman, but he wasn't buying. 'You don't strike me as the mercenary type.'

Allegra blinked as if she were fighting tears.

'Why don't you tell me about it?' He reached out and took her hand in his.

Allegra looked away as she bit her lip. 'I wanted to help a friend. She desperately wanted to have children but couldn't. I had ovaries I wasn't going to do anything with and wanted money to start my design business. It seemed like a deal made in heaven.'

'What happened? You didn't start your design business?' Emmett rubbed circles on Allegra's palm, trying to soothe her pain through his touch.

'I never got the money. My boyfriend at the time had plans of rock stardom and absconded with the cash. So I ended up with no money, no friend, and now I have a 13-year-old who expects a maternal figure and instead has me.'

'Don't underestimate yourself. You don't have to be perfect, you just have to be there.' Emmett knew that all too well. When he first became Rhys' guardian, every day had been a battle until he realized, with the help of a therapist, that Rhys was pushing the boundaries to see whether Emmett would abandon him the way he felt both his parents had. Rhys had struggled to process his mother's dementia and the fact that she forgot him. All he knew was that the mother who had loved and taken care of him suddenly wasn't living with him anymore, and the brother he didn't remember sharing a roof with was now acting like his parent.

'Do you want children?' she asked.

'That was the plan,' Emmett said. 'But plans change. Now, all I can think about is taking care of Rhys.'

'You're still young,' Allegra said.

'I'm 31. Old enough to know that life throws you unexpected curve balls, and you just have to catch them. Being a parent may or may not be in the cards for me, and I'm not worried one way or another.'

'Your fiancé was crazy to let you go,' Allegra said, bringing him back to the present.

Emmett smiled. 'You say all the right things.'

'No, you're quite a catch.'

Emmett felt himself sit up straighter as confidence filled him. It had been so long since a woman looked at him with desire in her eyes. His eyes drifted to her lips, and he leaned forward and kissed her, keeping his arms by his side so that only their lips touched.

'Do you want a tour of the mansion?' Allegra murmured against his lips.

He pulled back and looked into her eyes. She was looking at him with curiosity. He knew she wanted him. Her eyes were half closed and her voice raspy, yet she was stopping them from taking it to the next level. He started leaning forward, desperate to join their lips again, to feel her body pressed up against him when he saw the pain in her eyes before she closed them. He remembered the disappointment in her voice when she told him she wanted them to be friends first.

'I would love a tour,' he said, even though every nerve ending in his body was screaming otherwise.

Allegra smiled at him with tenderness, and he felt relief. He'd made the right decision.

Allegra led him upstairs, where the rooms were empty and in need of some tender loving care.

'As you can see, I've only been able to refurbish one room.' She walked into the bedroom, and he followed. 'The previous owners left this here. I just freshened it up.' She pointed to the gigantic vintage four-poster bed with an antique tufted headboard.

He noticed the mirror vanity with hairbrushes and knick-knacks on top of it. The wall mirror had lights placed around it. 'Is this your bedroom?'

When she nodded, he had to turn away from the bed to hide his reaction. All he could think about was all the ways and positions he could make love to Allegra on that gigantic bed.

'Henry was the one who introduced me to Lebop,' Allegra said as they walked down the stairs and into the ballroom that doubled as her dance studio.

'Lebop?'

'Yes, it's a modern style jive. I'll give you a lesson.' She started the music and led him through the moves.

As they danced, Emmett felt himself relax. He appreciated why these types of dances were popular. It was all about seduction, and he felt seduced. He took her in a turn, and she flipped around. When she stopped, her face was under his. It was the most natural thing in the world to lean down and kiss her on the lips. He picked her up and put her on the free-standing bar in the corner of the room, sliding between her thighs. His hand moved across her back and finally touched the bare skin that was tormenting him. The halter tie tickled his fingers, and he clutched it in his hand, tugging on it. He moved away and watched Allegra's face as he untied the halter neck and pushed the front of her dress down. He leaned forward and kissed her neck, working his way down the front of her body and to the tops of her breasts in the black brassiere. Her breasts were plump and crying out for his hands. He cupped them, and they fit perfectly in the palm of his hands.

'Wait.' Allegra placed her hands on his. 'We were going to take it slow.'

He had to fight the instinct to kiss her until she forgot. She was panting, her eyes wide with desire. She was just as aroused as he was. He shifted and pressed his erection against the apex of her thighs. She moaned, closing her eyes as she leaned her head back, giving herself to him. All he had to do was kiss her again and he would sweep away her reservations, but he didn't want to do that. He wanted her to give herself to him willingly and without reservations.

He lifted her halter neck dress with shaking hands and tied the ribbon around her neck. 'I want this to be more than a moment of passion.' He stepped away and lifted her down from the bench. 'It's time for me to leave.'

He walked to the kitchen and got his jacket, holding it over his shoulder with his finger. 'I had a wonderful night.' He embraced her around the waist and walked with her to the front door. He kissed her until they both had to come up for air. 'I'll call you.'

She stood on the front stairs watching him as he walked to his car, and he had to fight the urge to go back, pick her up in his arms, and carry her upstairs, where he would ravish her until they both screamed their pleasure, but he was determined that he would do this right. He would woo and court Allegra until she wanted him as much as he wanted her.

Chapter 11

'What do you think about this?' Joleen asked, holding up a bolt of material. As Joleen was, in her own words, a girl with a special figure, she needed a special custom wardrobe, and Allegra was going to make her a few summer dresses. They bartered their services, Joleen helped Allegra with renovations, and she was her seamstress.

'That would make you look like an eggplant,' Allegra said, looking at the dark purple hue.

Usually, a material shop was her favorite place to be. She was so inspired when surrounded by bolts of fabric and imagining her new creations, and Joleen was a dream model. Making a flirty summer dress that would compliment her had inspired her sketches, and she had pages of design ideas, yet somehow she wasn't feeling her usual joie de vivre. Instead, she felt flat and testy.

'Gees, don't hold back,' Joleen said, returning the fabric to the stack she'd found it in. 'Don't get me wrong, but you seem to be a bit crabby. Anything wrong?'

'No, nothing,' Allegra said, sliding her hands over the white satin fabric. It felt so smooth under her hand, it felt like she was caressing skin. Her palms tingled, and her skin broke out in goose pimples at the tactile sensation of fabric as she imagined two nude bodies writhing in a bed of satin sheets.

'Because it seems to me like you're out of alignment. Maybe you need the Jackhammer of Delight?' Joleen lifted an eyebrow.

Allegra gave her a dirty look. Joleen was using their euphemism for a vibrator, and Allegra was annoyed, mostly because she was right. It had been two weeks since Emmett had embarked on his slow courtship. They had a date twice a week and had dinner, long conversations, some heavy petting, and then when things were getting heated, Emmett would get up and leave.

While she was the one who had wanted to take it slow and get to know each other, she was suffering serious withdrawal. It was only now that she was abstinent for a protracted period that she realized that sex was a biological imperative, at least for her. She didn't get any respite, and even her dreams were over-sexed and featured technicolor fantasies of her having sex with Emmett, sex with faceless men, orgies with heaving bodies and thrusting pelvises.

She'd dreamed every possible sexual combination in her dreams, and every morning woke aching and unfulfilled.

'You want to talk about it?' Joleen asked.

'No.' Allegra walked around and picked up another bolt of fabric embroidered lace that she stroked again.

'Stop molesting the fabric,' Joleen said, taking it from her.

Allegra looked around to see if anyone had noticed her strange behavior. Thankfully, everyone was occupied with their own shopping and hadn't noticed anything amiss. She walked over to the sewing patterns table.

'I've been taking it slow with Emmett,' Allegra said, lowering her voice so that others wouldn't notice as she picked up a sewing pattern. 'And I'm struggling with the whole 'no sex' bit.' As she spoke, she crumpled the packet in her hands.

'So life in the slow lane is not for you.' Joleen took the pattern from her and carefully smoothed down the paper before returning it to the rack.

Allegra gave her a look of agreement.

'What are you going to do about it?' Joleen asked.

Allegra looked at her in confusion.

'You're the one who wanted to take it slow, and Emmett has just been giving you what he thinks you want. Now it's time for you to change speeds.'

'Oh,' Allegra said as she realized Joleen was right.

At first, she'd wanted to see whether she and Emmett could have a different type of relationship than one she'd ever had before and develop true intimacy. They had spent hours together, getting to know each other. She had her best friends, Maree and Joleen, and they had true intimacy because there was no sex involved. She hadn't ever had that with a heterosexual male that she was attracted to until she met Emmett.

But now, she wanted their relationship to go to another level. She missed sex. She missed orgasms. And she'd even retired her plastic lover because it had felt too much like interfering with the natural energy between her and Emmett.

'Tonight is the night,' Allegra said. 'We need to go shopping.'

'That's what I'm talking about,' Joleen said, slapping Allegra on the butt as they walked out of the material shop.

Later that night, Allegra was sitting in front of her vanity, putting on the finishing touches to her hair, when she heard Emmett knocking. She had spent a good 2 hours preparing for tonight. First, she had a scented bath, then slathered herself in lavender body lotion, and only then began her hair and makeup. She took one last look in the mirror and smiled. At least getting dressed had taken no time.

She walked down the stairs slowly, feeling like her joints were loose and limber as if she'd spent hours on the dance floor. She opened the door, and Emmett looked her up and down with surprise, admiring her floor-length silk nightgown, the folds swirling around her so that it looked like she was walking on a silk cloud. His eyes caught on the lace of her bust. She was bra-less, and her nipples beaded from the breeze outside, making them thrust out through the lace.

'Sorry,' she said breathlessly. 'I lost track of time.'

Allegra turned and began walking back to the stairs so he could admire the back of the nightgown. It had an open back, and the deep-v dipped to just above the curve of her buttocks.

'I'll just go upstairs and get dressed,' Allegra said, looking over her shoulder. Emmett's eyes were on her *derriere*, the nightgown's cascading train swaying as she walked. She waited for his eyes to catch hers and let her desire show.

His hand reached for her in slow motion, and he roughly tugged her back. She stopped herself from falling by resting her hands on his chest, feeling the movement of his muscles under his shirt as he grasped her. His hands rested on her bare back, and she gasped at his cool hands resting on her hot flesh. She lifted her head and moaned with pleasure as his lips descended onto hers.

She felt his erection pressing against her and wanted him inside her. Her fingers grasped his shoulders and tugged him harder against her as her pelvis ground up against him. He lifted his head and looked at her in surprise. She was sick of the waiting game and wasn't going to give him the chance to pause their lovemaking again. Her hands tugged on his tie and pulled it off, throwing it onto the floor. Her hands greedily made their way to his shirt buttons, and she ripped them open, pressing herself up against his bare chest as they kissed again.

He put his hands under her buttocks and lifted her up against him. Her legs curled around his waist, and she moaned again as she felt his erection pressing against her. He started climbing the stairs, but she couldn't wait. Her hands moved to his belt buckle, and she undid it. He stopped on the stairs and dropped her legs as she undid his belt and pulled it out of the loop. She undid his zip, and her hand went into his pants until she enveloped his hardness in her hand.

He moaned and pulled her hand away. Emmett sat on the stairs and pulled her down on his lap, her legs on either side of him. He pulled the lace nightgown off her shoulder and licked her nipple. She grabbed hold of his head, her hands tugging on his hair as she pulled him closer, urging him to take her breast in his mouth. As he sucked her nipples, her head leaned back, and she panted as she ground herself on his lap. He placed his hand on her ankle and pushed up the nightgown. She bit her lip as she reveled in the slow glide of his hand, the gentle tickling of silk all combined into an erotic delight. He reached her thighs and lifted her as he pulled the nightgown around her waist.

'Oh God,' he moaned as his hands reached her naked buttocks, and he realized she wasn't wearing any underwear.

Allegra felt him pressing against her entrance, and with a tilt of her pelvis, he was inside. They both moaned as their flesh merged. He turned around and lay her back against the stairs, protecting her head with his hand.

She held her legs around his hips and urged him in. He withdrew and pushed back, the delicious friction making her desire more. She put her hands on his buttocks and urged him to go harder. Their moans rent the air. It was fast and furious, and a few minutes later she was clenching her thighs around him as delicious contractions swept over her. She gasped with delight as she gently bit his shoulder.

'Are you okay?' he asked, sitting up and taking her with him. His hand gently smoothed her hair back as he looked into her eyes.

'I'm fabulous,' she said with a smile. 'Do you want to try it in a bed?'

He laughed. 'All right.'

She stood and pulled down her nightgown. He pulled up his pants, doing up the zip. She held out her hand and walked him upstairs. He looked impossibly gorgeous with his torso bare and his pants riding low on his pelvis.

They got to the bedroom, and she led him to the bed before sinking to her knees and, undoing his zip and pulling his pants down. He stepped out of his pants, and she threw them across the room. Her hands rubbed his hairy thighs, loving the friction of his rough skin on her palms as she slowly felt her way to his underwear and then pulled them down. He took her arm and pulled her up when she had tugged them off. He pushed her straps off her shoulder, and her nightgown fell to the floor. He took her hand and led her to the bed, lying down with her. They lay on their side, their torsos against each other. She expected him to kiss her, but he lifted her hand to his lips and began by kissing her fingertips. He kissed her fingers, then her wrist, and moved his way up her arm.

'This time, I'm going to treasure you,' he said and did just that.

He used his hands, his fingers, and his tongue to worship her body. He brought her to the edge, and when she was begging for him, he entered her and slowly rocked her to an orgasm.

Afterward, they lay under the covers, her head on his shoulder while his arm curved around her buttocks.

'God, I needed that.' Allegra kissed his chest.

'You did?' he said with surprise.

'Why are you surprised?' She lifted her head and looked at him.

'I just didn't think that women were wired the same as guys,' Emmett said, his hand gently caressing her back.

'Some women might not be, but I am. Having sex was like committing a community service because I was becoming monstrous.' She lay her head back down. 'What about you? Weren't you suffering?'

'Oh, yes, I was.' Emmett's voice was full of relief.

She felt his erection against her stomach and laughed.

'As you can see, he's gone into hyperdrive.' He looked at his watch. 'I think we've officially missed our reservation.'

Her stomach growled. 'Damn, I've got nothing in the fridge,' Allegra said, remembering she'd neglected to go grocery shopping.

'I guess we'll have to do a fast food run.'

They sat up in bed together. He kissed her on the nose, and Allegra got out of bed. Emmett leaned against the headboard and watched her. She enjoyed the way his eyes possessively moved over her body as she walked to her wardrobe. She perused her clothes before choosing a dress and carrying it to her vanity, where she hung it on a wall hook. He watched her put on a slip, re-do her hair, and update her makeup.

Usually, she would leave the room and not let her lover observe her routine because it was too intimate, but Emmett was different. She didn't feel self-conscious about letting him see her as anything less than perfect, a novel sensation for her.

'Can you do it up for me?' she asked after she slipped on her dress.

He stood, his erection bobbing as he walked toward her.

'What if I want to take it off again?' he asked as he leaned forward and nuzzled her neck.

'You can,' she whispered. 'But I won't have much energy without food.'

She smiled at him in the mirror as he did the zipper. He turned her around, and they swayed together in a romantic daze. It was so much more erotic that he was naked and she was dressed. He picked up her hand and kissed it before finding his underwear and putting it on.

They walked downstairs, looking for his clothes and giggling as they found his tie in the living room.

When he was dressed, they went to a local Chinese restaurant and ate, punctuating their bites with frequent kisses and touches. She drove them back and stood by his car.

'I wish I didn't have to go,' he said, hugging her.

'Me too,' she whispered.

He had to be home by 12 o'clock. It was like he was Cinderella and would turn into a pumpkin, but instead of a Fairy Godmother, his babysitter dictated to him.

Allegra went into the house and waved from the window, feeling a furious mix of joy and sadness. She couldn't wait to see him again.

Chapter 12

Emmett tried to concentrate on the staff meeting he was in, but he couldn't stop thinking about Allegra and their night together. He'd spent the past two weeks having cold showers after each date with Allegra, the sexual desire building until he thought he'd burst, but he'd been determined to wait until she was ready for him.

He saw Imogen looking at him with a questioning look and realized he was smiling as he stared into space. He frowned and looked back at the head of the table where his boss was updating them about their caseload.

An hour later, the staff meeting was over, and Emmett returned to his office. 'How are you going, buddy?' he asked Rhys, who was sitting at his meeting table on his laptop. It was a planning day at his school, and Betty wasn't available during the day, so Rhys worked with Emmett.

'Good.' Rhys barely looked up from the screen.

'What are you working on?' Emmett leaned forward and looked at the screen. Rhys was chatting with Amethyst. 'That doesn't look like homework.'

'That's where you'd be wrong,' Rhys said, typing 'BRB' before turning to look at him. 'I'm working on a science project with Amethyst.'

'Oh, okay,' Emmett said. 'I'm going to the kitchen. Do you need anything?'

'A juice would be good,' Rhys said, his fingers feverishly clicking away.

Emmett was making himself a coffee in the kitchen when Imogen walked in. She slowed when she saw him and nodded hello. Emmett nodded back and stared at his cup, willing the coffee machine to drip faster. It was very awkward to be working with your former fiancé, but those were the breaks.

'How have you been, Emmett?' Imogen asked as she took out a juice from the fridge.

'Good, and you?' Emmett asked.

'Great.' Imogen took a glass from the cupboard near his head and poured the juice, her diamond ring glittering in the light.

Emmett didn't feel the usual punch in the guts when he saw her engagement ring, the proof that she'd replaced him in her life within a month of their breakup. Maybe it was true, and time really healed.

'How is Rhys?' Imogen asked.

Emmett gave her a look. The last time she'd seen his brother had been a month before. Imogen's niece had run away from home, and Imogen had found an email from Rhys and showed up on his doorstep hysterical as she demanded answers from his brother. Rhys had clammed up and hid himself in his room. He'd been so distraught that he'd missed school the next day and had to see a doctor who doubled up on his anxiety medication to get him functional again.

'Fine, thanks for your concern.' Emmett's coffee had finished, and he grabbed the cup, the hot liquid spilling on his hand. He refused to wince, and pain and anger swirled inside him as he walked away.

'I'm sorry I upset him,' Imogen said. 'I was distraught that Amethyst was lost, and I kept picturing her hurt and alone.'

Emmett turned slowly. 'As always, Imogen, the end justifies the means for you.'

'That's not fair,' Imogen said. 'Those were extenuating circumstances. I'm Amethyst's guardian. She has only me to protect her.'

Emmett raised an eyebrow. In the last year of their relationship, those were words that Emmett had spoken to her frequently, and yet there had been no understanding or sympathy on her part.

Imogen had the grace to flush with embarrassment.

Emmett turned toward the fridge. He smiled as he took a sip of his coffee. Maybe he'd been wrong all along, and karma really did exist. He took an orange juice from the fridge and poured it into a glass. He got five blocks of ice and put them in.

Imogen began walking out of the kitchen carrying her coffee but stopped at the doorway. He looked up in exasperation, about to snap, only to catch himself when he saw her face was wet with tears. He'd never seen her cry in the five years they'd been together.

'I'm sorry. I wasn't understanding about Rhys at all. In fact, I think I was a bitch, and I couldn't see your point of view at all.'

She quickly wiped her face and walked out. Damnit, now he felt like a bastard for being so harsh. He'd just spent so long being angry at her for the way things ended. While he didn't blame her for not wanting to take on the responsibility of Rhys, it was a big ask after all. He blamed her for how things had ended, but maybe it was time to let go of the grudge. They worked together, after all, and now that he'd met Allegra, his anger was easing. He took a deep breath and picked up his coffee and Rhys' drink. Maybe he needed to tamp down his anger and play nice with her. He returned to his office, gave Rhys his drink, and settled into work.

Rhys stood and headed for the door.

'Where are you going?' Emmett asked.

'Toilet.'

'Okay, but go there and back. I don't want you distracting anyone from their work.' His boss didn't have any problems with Rhys coming to the office, and Emmett didn't want that to change.

Emmett was just about to go looking for him when Rhys returned fifteen minutes later. 'What took you so long?' he asked.

'I was speaking to Imogen.' Rhys sat down at his computer.

'What about?' Emmett asked, surprised that Rhys had voluntarily spent time with Imogen. When they dated, Rhys and Imogen's relationship had gone from lukewarm politeness to animosity.

'She wanted to apologize for how she was last time. She said she was worried about Amethyst and not thinking clearly, and if she had, she knew I wouldn't have done anything to hurt my friend.'

'Oh,' Emmett was surprised. This was a side of Imogen he hadn't expected. Maybe she had been sincere about wanting to bury the hatchet. He would see her before he left for the day, tell her they could try being friends.

He finished work for the day and remembered that he had to see Imogen.

'I'll be back in a few minutes, and then we'll leave,' he told Rhys as he left his office.

As he approached Imogen's office door, he heard raised voices.

'You'll just have to find a babysitter,' a male voice said. 'She's not my kid, and I've had enough of changing my life for her.'

Another voice spoke, but it was quieter, and Emmett couldn't hear it through the door.

'That's your problem, not mine.' The door opened, and Imogen's fiancé, Greg, burst past Emmett.

Imogen called Greg's name and appeared in the doorway. She saw Emmett, and her face flushed. She quickly wiped her face. 'I'm sorry you had to hear that.' She turned her back and got some tissues off her desk.

'Are you all right?' Emmett asked.

Imogen turned and looked at him with a sad smile. 'That's very kind of you to show concern,' Imogen said, 'but I don't want to keep you. Why were you coming to see me?'

'It was actually about our conversation earlier,' Emmett said. 'I wanted to say that I have been unnecessarily harsh toward you.'

'Maybe you haven't,' Imogen said. 'Now that I'm on the other side of the conversation, I want to slap myself across the face. I spent all those months thinking only about how my life was changing and had absolutely no sympathy for what you were going through.'

'It's okay,' Emmett said. 'Sometimes you only know things after you've been through them.'

'That's very kind of you,' Imogen said, 'but all I needed to do was show a little empathy, and my life would have been completely different.'

Their eyes caught for a moment, and he realized she truly regretted the end of their engagement. He imagined what his life would have been like if only she had known then what she knew now. They would have been married as they had planned, and when Imogen's brother died and she became Amethyst's guardian, her niece would have just become another family member. Their lives would have continued as planned, but then he wouldn't have met Allegra. He realized maybe things had turned out for the best after all.

'Karma is a bitch,' he said.

Imogen looked at him in shock before laughing.

'That could have gone either way,' Emmett said as he laughed with her.

'Thank you,' Imogen said, her face softening.

'I'll see you tomorrow.' Emmett started walking away but hesitated and turned back. 'Did you need a babysitter?' he asked.

Imogen looked at him with hope.

'I've got a date tonight, and Betty is watching Rhys. If you like, you can drop Amethyst over.

They could probably use some face-to-face time to work on their science project together.'

'Science project?' Imogen frowned.

'Yes, they've been messaging each other to-day about it.'

'Oh, I didn't know.' Imogen looked sad before forcing a smile. 'I guess I have a way to go before I become Amethyst's confidante.'

'It takes time,' Emmett said.

'Thanks. You are a lifesaver.'

'That's okay. As long as the kids are happy.' Emmett stepped away. 'I'll see you tonight.'

Imogen nodded and smiled.

Emmett walked away, surprised at how his day had turned out. He'd started it with Imogen firmly in the enemy camp. He hadn't thought there would be a scenario where he would be willing to forgive and forget, but being a par-ent meant putting someone else's needs above your own. Rhys didn't have many friends, and Emmett was glad that Amethyst was back in his life, and if that meant having to see Imogen socially occasionally, then he would just have to live with it.

***

Emmett knocked on Allegra's door. He'd spent the day desperately counting the minutes until he could see her again. She opened the door, and he saw his desire mirrored in her eyes. He reached for her, and they kissed, and somehow, they kept their lips joined as they climbed the stairs, losing clothes as they went. Emmett picked her up in the bedroom and lifted her onto the bed. He looked down at her, loving the feel of her near-nude body under his. He wanted to savor this moment, but then she wrapped her legs around his and flipped him over so that she was on top. She took charge, and he reveled in her abandon as she rode him until they both orgasmed.

Afterward, she lay on his shoulder, and he covered them with a sheet.

'I've been thinking about this all day,' she said, gently caressing his chest.

Emmett smiled, feeling triumphant. A cell phone ringing rent the air.

'Is that yours?' he asked as they sat up.

Allegra shook her head. 'Mine's downstairs.'

Emmett got out of bed. 'Sorry, it might be about Rhys.'

Allegra nodded and sat up against the headboard.

He looked at the screen and wanted to curse. 'Betty, what's wrong?' he asked when he answered.

'Rhys is fine. It's my granddaughter. She broke her arm and is in the hospital.'

'You go to the hospital. I'll be there in 15 minutes,' he told Betty and hung up. 'I'm sorry,' he said to Allegra as he found his underwear and pulled them on, telling her what was happening.

'Is her granddaughter all right?' Allegra got out of bed, found her dress, and put it on.

'I'm not sure.' Emmett dressed as he walked downstairs. He couldn't find his left shoe and walked toward the kitchen, finding it in the doorway. He glanced inside and saw she'd set the table. His nostrils flared as he smelled lobster.

'I wasn't taking any chances this time,' Allegra said, appearing beside him. 'So I ordered lobster bisque.'

'It smells delicious,' Emmett said, his stomach rumbling.

'Here, I'll pack some for you to take,' Allegra said, opening a kitchen cupboard and taking out a container.

'Why don't you come over, and we can all have it together?' He took her hand and held it. He didn't want their date to end.

Allegra smiled. 'I'll follow you in Ruby.'

'Who's Ruby?'

Allegra smiled as she quickly packed up their dinner. They walked out together to the garage. Emmett felt his jaw drop as Allegra lifted the garage door, and a 1957 Cadillac appeared.

'This is one beautiful baby,' he said, caressing the shiny exterior.

'Be careful, a girl could be jealous of her car with that look in your eyes.' Allegra opened the passenger door and carefully placed the bag with the containers on the seat.

Emmett sighed and went to his car. Allegra started up the Cadillac and followed him to his house.

When they arrived, he walked inside and saw Amethyst and Rhys sitting on the couch, each holding their laptops, and realized he'd forgotten about her presence. Damnit, it was going to be awkward when Imogen came.

Emmett turned toward Allegra as she came in and began introductions.'You know Rhys, and this is his friend-'

'Amethyst,' Allegra finished the sentence.

'The two of you know each other?' Emmett asked. Allegra looked shocked and nervous while Amethyst was smiling with delight.

'This is the girl I was telling you about,' Allegra said.

Emmett drew a blank.

'She's my egg donor,' Amethyst said, filling the awkward silence.

'That's right.' Allegra said. 'I'm her egg donor.'

'Oh, okay,' Emmett said, completely out of his depth. He didn't know what to say but could see that Allegra was even more thrown than him. 'We brought dinner?' Emmett took the bag from Allegra as he caught the frantic look in her eye.

'We'll go get it ready. Just through here,' he said, leading her into the kitchen.

'That was bad, wasn't it?' Allegra demanded after he closed the door. 'That was terrible the way I hesitated. I just didn't know what to say.' She looked at him with a pleading face.

'That's fine. You dealt with it all right.' He put the bag on the kitchen counter as he tried to process the tangled connections. 'So if you're Amethyst's egg donor, that means you know Imogen?'

'I know her, and I wish I didn't. Hold on, how do you know Imogen?' she asked.

The doorbell rang, and Emmett heard voices.

'Imogen's here,' Rhys shouted.

'Just a minute,' Emmett shouted. 'There's something you need to know before we go out there.' He took hold of Allegra's elbow. 'Imogen is-'

The kitchen door opened, and Imogen appeared. 'What is she doing here?' she asked, catching sight of Allegra.

'Allegra is my date,' Emmett snapped, cursing the fact that he'd ever thought anything good could come of inviting your ex into your life. 'And this is Imogen, my former fiancé.'

Allegra looked at him in shock, obviously trying to process the bombshell.

Imogen turned to look at Allegra, and her face tightened in annoyance. 'Is this a joke?' she demanded while looking at Allegra. 'Are you trying to cause trouble by dating my former fiancé?'

'If he's your former fiancé, then it's none of your business who he dates,' Allegra said.

'I doubt it was his choice,' Imogen said. 'Emmett, dear, this is the creature I was telling you about. The one who is Amethyst's egg donor.' She turned back to Allegra. 'I told you I don't want you in Amethyst's life. And I don't know what you're trying to pull, but I won't have your trouble making.' She looked at Emmett. 'I must insist that you never see her again.'

Emmett noticed Amethyst and Rhys peering in through the doorway.

'Insist. Isn't that interesting? And how do you feel, Emmett, having your former fiancé make demands of you?' Allegra asked with a smile.

'Now isn't the time,' Emmett said, nodding toward the doorway. 'We are causing a scene.'

Imogen looked around in chagrin, smoothing her hair behind her ear. 'This conversation isn't over.' She gave Allegra a hard look. 'Thanks for offering to babysit Amethyst,' she said, kissing Emmett on the cheek.

Emmett walked Imogen and Amethyst to the door.

'We'll talk about this tomorrow,' Imogen said at the door.

Emmett was happy to close the door behind her, leaving his hands on the wood as he took a moment to figure things out. How could this have happened? How is it that Allegra was Amethyst's egg donor, but he knew nothing about it? The whole thing seemed slightly strange.

'What happened?' Rhys asked, bringing him back to the present. 'Why were Allegra and Imogen fighting?'

'It's complicated,' Emmett said. 'Can you please go to your room so Allegra and I can talk privately?'

'But I want to know what happened,' Rhys said.

Allegra came out of the kitchen. 'I'm afraid that's my fault. Imogen and I know each other, and we don't like each other very much.'

'That's okay, I don't like Imogen either,' Rhys said. 'Good night, Allegra.'

'Good night, Rhys.' She waited until Rhys left the room. 'I should probably get going.'

'We need to talk,' Emmett said, surprised she was so eager to leave.

'I don't know if that's a good idea.' Allegra lifted her hand handbag to her shoulder, her hand clinging tightly to the strap.

'Are you angry?' Emmett asked, taking stock of her face. Her lips were thin, and she was frowning. Why was she angry? He was the one who had cause to be angry. She hadn't told him Amethyst's name, and if she had, this whole thing could have been avoided.

'Yes, I am. Your ex-fiancé demanded that you don't see me again, and you said nothing to contradict her.' She threw her handbag on the couch.

'That's not true.' Emmett approached her slowly as he realized how it looked from Allegra's point of view. 'It wasn't the time. Rhys and Amethyst were listening to the argument.' He placed his hands on her arm gently. 'Imogen is in my past, and nothing she says or does has any influence on my life.' It surprised him she was being so insecure. She should know what she meant to him.

'But why was Amethyst here? Imogen said you offered to babysit her.' She tilted her head to look at him.

Damn, Imogen and her big mouth. She was always eager to score points and didn't care about the mess she left behind.

'Yes, I did, because Rhys and Amethyst are friends and are working on a science project together.'

'She made it sound like you were doing it to get close to her,' Allegra said.

'That's not true,' Emmett said. 'The only reason I did it was for Rhys, but it's probably best if I avoid another fiasco like that.'

'Yes, having some distance from Imogen will be good.' Allegra stepped closer and lay her head on his chest.

He put his arms around her waist and held her. He hated to ruin the moment, but he had to tell her the whole truth and not have anything else hanging over him. 'There's something else I need to tell you. Imogen and I work together.' He held himself stiffly as he waited for a reaction.

'Oh,' Allegra said without lifting her head to look at him.

'But our work relationship is strictly professional, and to be honest, most of the time, we hardly see each other,' Emmett quickly added, hoping to forestall any issues.

'As long as that's the case.' Allegra tilted her head up, and he kissed her.

'I thought that was going to be more of a problem,' Emmett said when their kiss ended, and they snuggled once again, his chin resting on her head. He stood with her, enjoying the silence. He couldn't believe that this night had turned out to be so full of drama, but at least everything between him and Allegra was good. Although something was nagging at him. 'Can I ask you something?'

'Sure,' Allegra murmured, and he felt the vibration of her voice against his chest.

'Why didn't you tell me you were Amethyst's egg donor?'

Allegra lifted her head and looked at him with confusion. 'I did.'

'You told me you were an egg donor, but you never told me Amethysts's name,' Emmett said, finding the omission strange.

'Of course not. I wasn't going to break Amethyst's confidentiality. After all, I knew that she and Rhys went to the same school and you might know her. You should understand better than anyone since you're a lawyer.'

'Of course,' Emmett said. It made sense. There would have been a confidentiality agreement in the contract that Allegra signed, and she was just being prudent with the information she shared. And yet, why did he still feel that something was off?

'Although it is strange.' Emmett lifted his head. 'The fact that we're all connected. I mean, if you were looking for a way to get under Imogen's skin, this was the perfect way.'

'Are you saying you believe I'm going out with you just to get at her?' Allegra had gone stiff in his arms, and he regretted his words as soon as he uttered them.

'Of course not,' Emmett said. 'I was just saying that the whole thing is strange.'

'If you remember, you were the one who asked me out.' Allegra moved out of his arms and walked to the couch, picking up her handbag. 'Maybe you're the one with the ulterior motive. Maybe you didn't ask Amethyst here because of Rhys but because you wanted to show Imogen that you had moved on.' Her eyes were flashing, and her cheeks were flushed.

He knew she had reason to be angry, but he was getting frustrated with the whole conversation. 'The only reason I'm going out with you is because I want you.' He pulled her back to him so they were pressed against each other. He could feel her small pants of breath on his lips. He wanted nothing more than to press his lips onto hers and make her feel the force of his desire. She licked her lips as she looked at him, and suddenly he knew. She wanted him to kiss her. He leaned in, but just before their lips touched, she pushed him away.

'Nice try, big boy,' she said, heading for the door.

'Please don't leave like this.'

She yanked the door open without replying and stalked down the stairs, her high heels creating a furious stat taco as she left.

Emmett closed the door and banged his forehead against it. What the hell was he thinking? He had a beautiful woman who desired him, and yet he'd somehow managed to blow it. How the hell was he going to fix this mess?

Chapter 13

Allegra woke to a knocking on the door. She covered her head with a pillow. She'd tossed and turned after her fight with Emmett and had only fallen asleep in the early hours of the morning. The knocking stopped, and she turned on her side and closed her eyes when her phone began ringing. She picked it up and saw it was Joleen. 'Ugh,' she groaned. Joleen would not give up without seeing her. 'Coming,' she said as she answered and promptly hung up.

She walked downstairs, her head feeling slightly achy. After she let Joleen in, Allegra headed for the kitchen. She needed caffeine.

'How did your date go last night?' Joleen asked as she followed.

'It didn't.' Allegra opened the coffee tin, feeling herself perking up as she greedily inhaled caffeine.

'What? Did he stand you up?' Joleen asked as she sat at the kitchen counter.

'No, no.' Allegra shook her head. She sighed as she spooned coffee and flicked on the coffeemaker. 'We had a date, but then it all blew up. Imogen is his former fiancé.'

'Imogen?' Joleen looked blank for a moment. 'You mean Elsa?' she asked as she frowned.

Allegra nodded. Joleen insisted on giving nicknames to those she disliked, and she'd dubbed Imogen the Snow Queen from Frozen after Allegra had shared their run-ins.

'Wow, how did Emmett and Elsa end up together? I'm really struggling with the mental image.' Joleen looked as shell-shocked as Allegra had felt after finding out last night.

'They were together for five years, and then she broke up with him when he became a guardian for Rhys.' Allegra felt a wave of sympathy as she remembered Emmett's face when he told her. Imogen had shattered his confidence to pieces after she chewed him up and spat him out.

'Damn, that's cold. Even for a Snow Queen.'

Allegra told Joleen about their date being interrupted and how she went back to Emmet's place, only for everything to blow up when she saw Amethyst and Imogen.

'So, Elsa thinks you're dating Emmett to get back at her?'

Allegra nodded as she stared at the coffee maker percolating. She felt soothed as it bubbled.

'She whacked.'

Allegra nodded again.

'Although it kind of is a perfect type of revenge, I mean, if you really wanted to get up her nose.'

Allegra gave her a dirty look. That's why she'd been so furious with Emmett when he'd mentioned it. There had been a part of her that had enjoyed thinking about Imogen's reaction when she knew they were together, but the other part had felt like crap because Emmett thought her interest in him was because of an ulterior motive. 'Yes, and Emmett thought that's why I was seeing him, too.'

'Did he say that?' Joleen asked.

'As good as,' Allegra said as she poured them a cup of coffee each. Allegra felt a prickle of guilt. She had to be honest. It gave her a bit of delight that Imogen's nose was bent out of joint about her dating Emmett. If she hadn't known about Emmett and Imogen, she wasn't sure she wouldn't have pursued the relationship for that reason only. Thankfully, her motives were never put to the test.

'That means he didn't say that, but that's what you heard.'

'So now I'm imagining things.' Allegra banged Joleen's cup down in front of her, making the coffee slosh out.

'No, but remember, I've had many an argument with a woman who heard something I didn't say,' Joleen said, getting a napkin and wiping her cup with it.

Allegra wanted to argue further, but Emmett had asked her not to leave the way she had, and yet she'd walked out into a huff. Sometimes it sucked being a drama queen, and sometimes it also really sucked having a best friend who used to be a man. Joleen would never give her unstinting sympathy because she always saw the male point of view. Allegra took a sip of her coffee as she brooded about what was really bothering her.

'There's something more,' Joleen said, narrowing her eyes as she looked at Allegra's face.

'No, there's nothing.' Allegra stood and went to the cupboard to find some biscuits to serve.

'I've got all day.' Joleen sat on the stool and smiled.

Allegra closed the pantry and leaned against it. 'Imogen and Emmett work together.'

'So?' Joleen asked, looking confused.

Allegra had had the opportunity to tell Emmett about her and Mark working together. He'd even given her an opening when he'd said that he was surprised at how well she'd taken the fact that he and Imogen worked together, but she hadn't told him. There had just been something in her that screamed danger, and she'd hesitated.

'Oh.' Joleen's face cleared. 'You didn't tell him about Mark.'

Allegra shook her head and sat back down at the kitchen counter.

'You're going to have to tell him sometime.' Joleen put her hand across her shoulders and hugged her.

'I know, but I just wanted more time for us to get to know each other before throwing that spanner into the works.' Allegra leaned her head on Joleen's shoulder. It felt like their whole date last night had exploded, and their relationship was hanging on a precipice. She'd been too scared to add one more bit of drama that might tip them over, so she'd done her usual. She'd picked a fight and run away in a huff so she wouldn't have to deal with it.

'Well, go and get yourself gussied up now, and I'll begin stripping back that wall.' Joleen stood and collected her toolbox from the hallway.

'And where am I supposed to be going?' Allegra asked.

'You're going to apologize to Emmett.'

'No, he should apologize to me.'

'Really?' Joleen quirked an eyebrow. 'He should apologize because you heard something he didn't say.'

'Well, yes,' Allegra said, knowing she didn't have a leg to stand on.

'Just remember, the longer you wait, the harder it is.' Joleen walked down the hallway to the back room that Allegra was renovating.

'I'm not apologizing,' Allegra shouted after her.

Allegra went upstairs, changed into her dungarees, and tied a headscarf around her hair before joining Joleen. This is just what she needed to get her mind off Emmett and their relationship drama. Joleen was using a steamer to steam the wallpaper while Allegra followed with the scraper, cleaning off the pieces of paper stubbornly stuck to the wall.

Renovating made her feel in control. She was achieving her dream and slowly returning this grand house to her glory. While it would be quicker if she had access to her trust fund and use the money to hire all the tradespeople she needed, she enjoyed being actively involved in the process rather than only being the check writer.

'You know, you won't even have to say sorry,' Joleen said, breaking their companionable silence. 'Just flash some cleavage, and he'll assume the rest.'

'I am not apologizing,' Allegra grunted as she ripped off the wallpaper.

They worked the rest of the day, and by 3 o'clock that afternoon, they stood in the middle of the room with their arms around each other, admiring the clean walls.

'Have you decided on a paint color?' Joleen asked.

Allegra shook her head. She was running low on cash and would have to wait a month until she could afford the paint. She'd scored another client as word-of-mouth spread and had two ball gowns and a pantsuit to make.

'I've got to pick up Lucas. Can you return the wall steamer?' Joleen asked as she put her tools into her toolbox. Lucas was Joe's son, and although they divorced, Joe had regular visitation.

'Sure,' Allegra said. She'd been able to forget about Emmett and all her troubles while renovating, but now that she had a breather, the realization that she had a free night to herself filled her with sadness.

'You know the hardware store is just near Emmett's office,' Joleen said, gently lifting her chin up. 'I'm sure seeing him would tilt that frown upside down.'

Allegra smiled sadly and said nothing as she walked Joleen out. She closed the door after Joleen and felt the empty house press around her. She knew Joleen was right, and she needed to talk to Emmett. Tell him about Mark so that he knew why her reaction was so off last night. She was just dreading the conversation. In her dating experience, men did not react well when presented with a potential rival, and that was when ultimatums happened. Usually, in past relationships, when things had come to such a sticky point, she had just bailed, not wanting to deal with the drama, but this time around, she wanted things to last, and she feared putting their relationship to the test.

There was only one thing for it. Allegra straightened and walked upstairs. She had to face this one head-on. Half an hour later, she looked at herself in the mirror and smiled seductively at her reflection. She was wearing a 1940s black pencil dress with a slit up to her thigh, a thick red belt that cinched in her waist, and a sweetheart neckline that showed off her cleavage. She hoped Joleen was right and that flashing some cleavage would do the trick.

Allegra returned the wall steamer to the hardware store before driving to Emmett's workplace. When she got up to reception, she asked for Emmett. A few minutes later, he appeared in the lobby.

'Allegra,' he said as he came over and kissed her on the cheek. 'This is a lovely surprise.'

She breathed in his scent, loving the feel of his five o'clock shadow on her cheek.

'I was hoping you had some time to talk.' Allegra was aware of the curious eyes of the receptionist watching them.

'Of course. Come to my office.' He put his hand on her waist and led her down the corridor.

She walked into his office and looked around curiously. It was a functional office with no personal knick-knacks. His desk was organized, and there was only one file on it, the pages neatly turned and a Newton's Cradle sculpture at the end. She'd obviously caught him in the middle of reading a contract.

'Please, sit down,' Emmett said as he closed the door.

He sat on the couch against the wall. Allegra knew he wanted her to sit next to him, but she leaned on the edge of the desk and cocked her hip slightly so that the leg slit went higher.

Emmett's eyes were drawn to her leg before returning to her face quickly. 'Listen, I was going to call you.' He put his hand through his hair. 'I didn't like the way our conversation ended yesterday.'

'What exactly was it you didn't like?' Allegra bent forward as she hit the Newton's Cradle, setting the collision balls to bounce off one another.

'I didn't like that we had our first fight,' he said.

'Neither did I.'

Emmett reached forward and stayed her hand before she set off the collision balls again. 'I'm sorry for what I said. It was very unfair.'

'Yes, it was,' Allegra said. 'I'm dating you for one reason and one reason only, because I like you.'

Emmett smiled, his face full of relief. He leaned forward, and they kissed. She knew she should stop the kiss and tell him about Mark. That's why she came after all, but she just wanted to revel in the moment. She sat on Emmett, her legs on either side of him, and kissed him hard. Soon, kisses weren't enough, and she began undoing the buttons of his shirt, her fingers slipping into the gap and caressing his skin.

'We shouldn't do this.' Emmett broke the kiss and whispered against her neck. 'Anyone can walk in.'

Allegra shivered as his breath blew on her neck. 'But doesn't that make it more exciting?' Allegra smiled at him and gently bit his lip.

He lifted her off his lap. She wanted to cry with disappointment. He walked to the door and flicked the lock.

'Now we don't have to worry.' He walked back and sat on the couch beside her, kissing her hard. Soon, she was lying under him while his hand slid up her leg and caressed her thigh.

Allegra closed her eyes as he inserted himself between her thighs and pushed up against her. It was so delightful to feel him pushing against her, and yet not being able to enter. She wanted him even more because of the tease factor. His finger lifted the edge of her underwear, and she wanted him to yank them off. Her hands went to his belt, and she started undoing it when there was a knock on the door.

Emmett stiffened on top of her. Their eyes met, and he cleared his throat. 'Who is it?' he called.

'It's me,' Imogen's voice said. She tried turning the handle. 'There seems to be something wrong with the door.'

'I'll be a moment.' Emmett got up and tucked his shirt in.

Allegra sat up and started giggling. Of course, it would be Imogen who would interrupt. She was the ultimate cock blocker. Allegra arranged herself on the couch. Emmett walked to the door and turned to check that she was decent before opening it.

'We need to talk,' Imogen said as she burst in. 'I've been in court all morning and wasn't able to see you earlier.' Imogen had eyes only for Emmett and hadn't noticed Allegra. 'You need to get that woman out of your life.'

'Does he now?' Allegra said.

Imogen's head snapped toward her.

'Hello Imogen,' Allegra said, waving at her.

Imogen's face flushed as she realized what she had walked into.

'I'm sorry. I'll come back later,' she said, heading for the door.

'No, I'd like you to stay.' Allegra stood. 'Emmett, would you give us a few minutes for some girl talk?'

'Why?' Imogen asked. 'He should stay. After all, this concerns him too.'

'Actually, it doesn't concern him at all. I'm here to talk about Amethyst. Anything else isn't your business.' Allegra walked over and kissed Emmett on the cheek. 'Give us ten minutes.'

Emmett nodded and headed for the door.

'So you're saying you're not dating Emmett just to get to Amethyst?' Imogen demanded before Emmett had even closed the door.

Allegra felt her face flush. 'You're forgetting a few things. One, I have a legal contract outlining that I can see Amethyst whenever I want. Two, if I want to take you to court to have custody of Amethyst, you and I both know that I have a good chance of succeeding. Therefore, I have absolutely no reason to involve Emmett in this.'

Allegra enjoyed watching Imogen's face blanch.

'You wouldn't try to take her away from me?' Imogen asked, her voice uncertain.

'I'm only interested in what's best for Amethyst, and if I ever conclude not living with you is not in her best interest, I will make sure she's taken care of.' Allegra felt a shock of fear go through her as she spoke the words, but she held herself steady in front of Imogen's disbelieving face. She hadn't planned on having this confrontation with Imogen. Hadn't planned on seeing her at all, but now that she was confronted with her, Allegra had gone on the attack. She realized that what she said was the truth. She'd gotten to know Amethyst in the past month and had developed a bond with her. She felt a responsibility to her and knew now that it bonded them for life. She would never abandon her and would make sure that Amethyst was taken care of.

'I knew you were after her,' Imogen said gleefully. 'The only reason you want her is because of her inheritance. I know what sort of woman you are. You're a gold-digger. You tricked Henry Brooks into leaving his mansion to you, even cutting out his own relatives from the will.'

'You were misinformed,' Allegra said, not surprised that Imogen had completed a background check and found out about Henry.

'No, I wasn't. Virginia and I are friends. She told me everything.'

Allegra paused. This was another spanner in the works, although she shouldn't be surprised. Imogen and Virginia were of the same ilk and probably attended the same country club.

'She told you wrong,' Allegra snapped, sick of being called a gold-digger. Taking a deep breath, she tried to contain her rage. She had to think about Amethyst and talk to Imogen calmly and rationally, even though she brought out the worst in her.

'I am asking you to please think about Amethyst. Think about what she's been through. She's lost both her parents, and she's looking for some sort of connection. I am not her parent. I will never be her parent, but I am a genetic link that she needs right now. You are her aunt. Nothing will ever change that. Can't we put our antagonism on the back burner and make her the focus? All I want is the opportunity for Amethyst to get to know me and for me to get to know her.'

Imogen looked at her mutinously for a moment before her face cleared. 'You're right. Perhaps I've been premature. Let's think about Amethyst.'

Allegra looked at Imogen suspiciously. She was saying all the right things, smiling charmingly, but Allegra couldn't help but feel that Imogen had given in too easily. She was up to something.

'Perhaps you should come over for dinner one night,' Imogen said.

Allegra hesitated. It was the last thing she wanted, but to refuse would be churlish. After all, if she wanted the best for Amethyst, then the two of them getting along would be best for her.

'Maybe,' Allegra said.

'This Saturday would be good.'

'I'm running a dance class,' Allegra said, feeling relief washing over her. In the past month, she and Mark had formed their new dance school and had delivered classes.

'We'll have to try for another night.'

'I'm booked up at the moment. I won't have a night off for a week at least.' It was an exaggeration, but Allegra needed time to process.

'I'll touch base with you later in the week.'

Allegra nodded, feeling like she'd wrestled with an Anaconda, and even though she was now escaping its grasp, she couldn't help but feel she was being toyed with and would soon fight for her life.

Emmett knocked on the door briefly before entering. 'Are you all right?' he asked Allegra, his face concerned.

'Everything is great,' Allegra said.

'I was just inviting Allegra over for dinner one night next week,' Imogen said.

'Great,' Emmett said, sounding uncertain.

'I'd better get going,' Allegra said, wanting to get away from Imogen.

'I'll walk you out.' Emmett nodded at Imogen as he walked past her. 'What happened?' he asked Allegra as he walked her to the elevator.

'I think we've called a truce.'

'I know I should be happy, but somehow knowing that my ex-fiancé and my current girlfriend will be friends makes me uncomfortable,' he said as he pressed the down button.

'That's the first time you said it.' Allegra smiled as joy filled her. 'You called me your girlfriend,' she clarified when he looked at her blankly.

'That's what you are.' He leaned down and kissed her on the lips. Just when things were getting steamed, there was a ring as the elevator arrived.

'Come over tonight,' Allegra said as she stepped on.

'You couldn't keep me away,' Emmett said.

The elevator closed, and she looked at the mirror on the wall beside her. She looked well kissed. She re-applied her lipstick and grinned at her reflection.

Chapter 14

Emmett returned to his office, his joy short-lived, when he saw Imogen was waiting for him. 'Excuse me, I have work to do.' He waited by the door for her to leave.

'Emmett, I'm worried about you.' Imogen placed her hand on his arm. 'I think she's using you.'

A co-worker passed by his office and looked in curiously. Emmett forced a smile and closed his office door. 'Why? You think a woman like that would only be interested in me if she had an agenda?' He felt anger take hold. She had already planted the idea last night, and he'd fallen for her mischief-making. He wouldn't do it again.

'Of course not.' Imogen looked at him with concern. 'I just wonder how much of her seeing you has to do with me and Amethyst.'

'Considering that you and I haven't been an item for a year, I really don't see how that would be the case,' Emmett snapped and walked to sit behind his desk, picking up the report he was reading before Allegra came.

'You shouldn't underestimate a woman like that.' Imogen walked over and leaned on the desk as she pleaded with him. 'Women who are from the wrong side of the tracks and will do anything to get ahead. Why don't you ask her about Henry Brooks and why he signed over his mansion to her, even cutting out his flesh and blood?'

'This is beneath you.' Emmett threw the report back on the desk. 'If there is anything Allegra wants to tell me, then she will.'

'Don't be naive. She has an agenda. She's trying to worm herself into your and Amethyst's life. Both of you are rich, and she most decidedly is not.' Imogen's voice was full of frustration.

'You mean naive like how I was with you,' Emmett hit back as his frustration built. 'Believing you when you said you wanted a break to sort out your feelings when you just needed time to lock down Greg Lancaster and his millions while keeping me on the hook.'

He'd never confronted her about their breakup, just taken it all in his stride and nursed the hurt. He'd even been willing to forgive and forget the past, but considering she was determined to interfere in his relationship with Allegra, she was due some home truths.

'That's not how it was.' Imogen looked shocked as she stood and stepped away from the desk. 'I just wasn't sure of my feelings.'

'So that's why I found out that our relationship was officially done when I saw your engagement announcement. Because you figured out your feelings just the moment he proposed.' He remembered the punch in his gut when he opened his morning paper and saw the article. When he'd tried talking to her about their break a few weeks before, she said she needed more time. He'd thought that meant she just needed a time out and that they would soon get their relationship on track. He hadn't realized that her feelings could change so quickly.

Imogen blinked away tears. 'I fell in love, and I'm sorry I hurt you, but I couldn't help my feelings. I tried to tell you we were over, but you just asked me to take more time to think it over. You wouldn't let me end it.'

Emmett rubbed his forehead as he tried to remember their last conversation. They'd been on a break for two weeks, and he'd seen her with Greg and started suspecting that they were more than friends. When he confronted her, she told him they both needed to move on. He remembered they had decided to take more time, but maybe he was the one who had told her to take more time rather than accepting the fact that they were over. He'd felt like his whole life was falling apart. His mother was in a nursing home, he was suddenly a full-time parent to a brother who had fought him at every turn, and the relationship that he'd thought was for life was suddenly stalling.

'Please, don't punish Amethyst for my mistakes,' Imogen was crying, her face distraught. 'I know you love your brother and will do anything for him, and that's how I feel about Amethyst. Please don't tell Allegra anything about me she could use against me.'

While he knew for a fact that Allegra had no underhanded motives in wanting to have a relationship with Amethyst, Imogen didn't know that. He knew she and Amethyst were struggling to get along, but that wasn't necessarily Imogen's fault. Rhys had tried to run away too when Emmett first took over parenting him. Emmett had spent the night at home, waiting for the police to call and hoping that when they did, they would have found him. Rhys had returned to their childhood home and spent the night sleeping on the back porch until the new owners discovered him. Emmett wondered how much worse his struggle would have been if there had been a rival for Rhys' affections.

'Of course, I won't say anything, but you need to know that you don't come up in our conversations.'

Imogen nodded and smiled in relief. 'And promise me if you find out anything that Allegra plans that might hurt Amethyst, you'll tell me.'

'I can't make that promise,' Emmett snapped. He couldn't believe he'd softened toward Imogen and given her a concession, only to have her step over a line again. She just didn't know when to quit.

'I know you don't know her, and you don't have loyalty, but I want you to think about Amethyst. She just lost her parents. She's vulnerable and seeking a connection, and she thinks that because she shares a genetic link with this woman, that makes her family. But that's not what family is. It's about being there over the years. She's my niece and I love her. I don't want her to end up getting hurt because of someone else's agenda.' She reached for his hand and held it as she pleaded. 'Please, Emmett, just promise me you won't think about me or about Allegra, that you'll think about Amethyst and how innocent she is. And that you'll help me protect her if she needs it.'

This wasn't the woman he had known. The Imogen he had been engaged to would have never pleaded with someone, no matter how important the issue. She really loved her niece and feared for her emotional well-being. He felt his frustration ease. She was irrational because she was consumed with fear. Maybe he needed to change tack.

'You have a completely different idea about Allegra.' He covered her hand with his. 'She's not interested in having children. She just wants to do the right thing by Amethyst because she was friends with her mother.'

Imogen raised her eyebrows, and her eyes widened. 'What do you mean, she was friends with Amy?'

Emmett was confused. 'Didn't you know that? She babysat Allegra when she was little.' He wondered momentarily why Allegra hadn't told Imogen about being friends with Amy, but quickly concluded that their conversations wouldn't have lent themselves to a heart-to-heart. Imogen had cast Allegra in the role of a villain and wasn't willing to shift from that position.

'That's not possible,' Imogen snapped. 'She was just an egg donor.'

Emmett felt a momentary disquiet. He hadn't meant to disclose something that Imogen didn't know. 'Perhaps you need to speak to Allegra about this.' He stepped away.

'Can't you see what a liar she is?' Imogen shouted. 'She's conning you. She and Amy didn't know each other.'

'You're the one who knows nothing. There is a photo of the two of them,' Emmett snapped back, having enough of her suspicion.

'Why haven't I seen it?' Imogen asked.

'I don't know and I don't care.' Emmett walked over to the door and opened it. 'This conversation is over.'

Imogen opened her mouth like she was going to argue, but she saw his face and thought better of it. She stalked out of his office, and he slammed the door closed.

He was going to have to tell Allegra about his confrontation with Imogen and that he'd told her about the photo. Emmett was also going to ensure he maintained his distance from Imogen. He was sick of the way he ended up being tied up in knots after each conversation with her. As he sat at his desk, he briefly wondered why Allegra didn't tell Imogen about the photo, but he assumed she had a good reason.

He got his coat and drove to Allegra's. This was an emergency, and barging in without a phone call was justified.

Chapter 15

Allegra was dancing with Mark. They were practicing a sultry dance when she looked up and saw Emmett standing in the doorway. She stiffened and stopped dancing abruptly. Mark looked at her with surprise as he side-stepped quickly, barely avoiding stepping on her foot.

'Sorry,' she said, collecting her towel from a side rail and dabbing at her sweat as she walked toward Emmett. 'I was expecting you later.' She kissed him on the cheek. It was 4 o'clock, and she was expecting him at 6 o'clock at least.

'I left work early so I could see you,' Emmett said.

'Is something wrong?' Allegra asked, noticing his tense face.

'I'll tell you later.' He nodded at Mark, who was approaching.

'Mark, this is Emmett.' Allegra introduced them.

'Did you want to finish up for today?' Mark asked after she'd performed introductions.

'Yes, please.' They were going to rehearse until 4.30, and then she was going to get ready for her date with Emmett, but they might as well call it a day.

'Nice to meet you, Emmett,' Mark said as he collected his bag.

Emmett nodded back.

'What is that you need to tell me?' Allegra asked.

'Imogen was waiting for me in my office after you left.'

'Let me guess, she only had nice things to say about me,' Allegra said wryly as she sipped from her drink bottle.

Emmett smiled faintly. 'During our conversation, Amy came up, and I told Imogen that the two of you were friends.'

Allegra slowly lifted her bottle away from her mouth and screwed the lid back on.

'She didn't know that until I told her.' Emmett looked at her questioningly. 'How did the two of you know each other?'

Allegra hesitated. All she had to do was tell him the truth. They were friends because their fathers were best friends, but if she did that, he would know her pedigree. Ever since she'd left home, she had told no one about who her parents were. She'd wanted to leave that life far behind, and since she hadn't access to her trust fund and had to work for a living like everyone else, it hadn't been difficult.

After Cole, she had wanted to ensure that anyone interested in a relationship or friendship with her was only doing so because of who she was as a person rather than her parent's net worth. Now that she was going to get access to her trust fund in a few months, her life would change in so many ways, but one thing she didn't want to give up was the peace of mind that she mattered more than her money.

'When I told Imogen about the photo, she insisted it was doctored,' Emmett said, interrupting her train of thought.

Allegra's ears sharpened. 'Do you agree with her?'

'No, of course not.' Emmett put his hands on her shoulder. 'I trust you. I know that you're not lying.'

Allegra put her hands on his chest as she looked into his eyes. He was completely sincere. She felt a weight lift off her chest. Of course, she didn't have to worry that Emmett's feelings would be influenced when he found out she was a trust fund baby. She opened her mouth to tell him the truth when he spoke.

'You know what I would really love to do.' Emmett leaned his forehead against hers. 'To stop talking about Imogen.'

Allegra smiled wickedly. 'I feel really sweaty,' she whispered against his lips. 'Would you like to help me bathe?'

Emmett's eyes darkened with desire. Allegra giggled and ran upstairs, Emmett in hot pursuit. She would tell him her secret later. There was no rush. He caught up with her in the bathroom. As she bent over to run the water in the claw bathtub, he pressed himself against her.

'Mr Dennison, how impatient you are,' Allegra said over her shoulder with a laugh.

'Yes, I am.' Emmett put his hand around her waist and helped her up, his hands cupping her breasts.

Allegra turned around and began undoing his buttons.

'No.' Emmett stilled her hands. 'I want to bathe you.'

She stood still as he slowly took off her clothes, his hands caressing her bare skin. He held her hand as she stepped into the bath. She lay back in the bathtub while he got a cloth and lifted her leg, washing her feet and calf. As his hand moved up her thigh, she gasped as his fingers gently brushed between her legs but didn't go further. He returned her leg gently to the water before washing her other leg. By the time he had finished bathing her whole body, she was limp with desire.

He helped her out of the bathtub and dried her gently before carrying her to bed, where he lay her down. He undressed while she watched him, her skin tingling. She lifted her arms and embraced him as he lay down on top of her. He kissed her deeply and inserted himself between her thighs, entering her in one swift thrust. She gasped as she wrapped her legs around him as he rocked them both to an earth-shattering orgasm.

Afterward, they lay together. Allegra's head was on his chest as he caressed her hair. She loved listening to the way his speeding heart-beat slowly returned to its regular rhythm.

'How long have you and Mark been dance partners?' he asked.

She knew this conversation was coming. 'For about eight months. Why?' She leaned on her elbow so she could look at him. 'Are you jealous?' she asked teasingly, wanting to introduce a light-hearted note into the conversation.

'No, as long as he knows you're not available.' Emmett lifted her other hand and kissed her fingertips.

'You don't have to worry about there being anything between us.' Allegra lay beside him and stared at the ceiling.

'Oh, good, he's gay.' Emmett sounded re-lieved.

Oh, no. It was happening. 'So if Mark were heterosexual, you'd be threatened?' she asked, wanting to give him an out.

'Not threatened, but concerned. The two of you get so close and intimate when you dance, and it would be very easy for one thing to lead to another.'

'You mean it would be easy for us to fall into bed together?' Even though Allegra had suspected that Emmett might have a problem with her dancing with Mark, she had thought that might be an issue *when* he found out that they were former lovers, not that he would just be threatened by the actual act of her dancing with another man.

'I guess, but you said I don't have to worry about it.'

She glanced over and saw that he was smiling. She couldn't wait to wipe the smile off his face. 'That's right. You have nothing to worry about because we already slept together.'

'What?' Emmett demanded, sitting up.

'Ouch.' Allegra sat up and tugged her hair out from under his arm.

'You two slept together?' he demanded.

Allegra nodded.

'How long ago?'

'A few months before we met.' She started feeling bad. He looked distraught at the thought. She'd gotten angry so fast she hadn't thought through how he would feel when he found out. 'The reason there's nothing to worry about is that we got over it, and now we're friends,' she said, putting her hand on his arm.

'What do you mean you got over it?' Emmett asked as he frowned.

'We burned the flame out, so to speak. The sexual spark was all there was between us, and it wasn't enough.'

'But you still dance together?'

'Yes, now our relationship is strictly professional.'

Emmett got out of bed and found his underwear. 'So one day you're a couple, and the next you're not,' he said as he yanked them on.

'We weren't ever really a couple in the strict sense.' Allegra kneeled on the bed, holding the sheet around her chest.

'What's the difference between being fuck buddies and a couple?' Emmett yanked on his pants, roughly zipping them.

'When you're a couple, you go out together. You go on dates. You talk and take an interest in each other like you and I did.' She got out of bed and followed him, holding the sheet around herself. 'but we were never like that. We used to go out in a group and rehearse and perform together, but we didn't really date.'

She had to get him to understand that what she and Mark had was just a shallow connection.

While she'd enjoyed having sex with Mark, it was nothing compared to what she and Emmett had.

'And I'm supposed to accept that the two of you can have this strictly professional relationship, even though your bodies are always pressed up against each other.' Emmett walked to the corner of the room where his shirt had landed when he took it off.

'Well, yes.' Allegra followed and stood in front of him, cornering him so he couldn't evade her. 'You're supposed to trust me. I'm with you and I'm going to be faithful.'

He hesitated, looking down at his shirt. Her hands tightened on the sheet as she waited for him to reply. *Please, please believe in me*, she begged inside.

He lifted his head and looked at her. 'I don't know if I can trust in that. What if the spark between the two of you returns one day, and you get back together?'

'That won't happen.' Allegra approached him slowly. 'I want to be with you.' She stood on her tiptoes and kissed his shoulder. 'I choose you.'

'Why don't you just get a new dance partner?'

'It's not that easy. Mark and I have a good partnership. I don't want to throw away all the rehearsal time, and now we've started our dance school.' She gestured with her hand, and her sheet dropped, exposing her nipple. 'It's like me asking you to get another job because Imogen works at your office.' She waited for Emmett to notice, but he was oblivious.

'That's different,' he said.

'How is it different?' she asked, lifting the sheet back up. 'The two of you are work colleagues. You see each other every day.'

'It's still different because we're not rubbing our bodies against each other.'

His face showed disgust. Allegra felt let down. To her, dancing was a way of expressing herself and reclaiming beauty in the world, but all Emmett saw was that it was sex on the floor.

'It's just dancing. It means nothing,' she whispered.

'So the sex you had with Mark means nothing, and dancing with him means nothing. How do I know that sex with me means something?' Emmett demanded.

'Because I told you. Because I showed you. I have never cheated on any of my lovers.'

'No, you just break up with one and daisy chain to another. Sometimes overnight.'

Allegra felt like he'd slapped her on the face. While what he was saying was the truth, that's exactly what she had done. She thought he understood she had changed. That she was a different person and, more importantly, what they had was special. But he didn't see any of that.

'You're right. That's exactly what I do.' She felt herself going cold, and her anger faded. She should have known that she couldn't escape her past. 'In fact, I think this is what I will do. As you say, out with the old, in with the new.' She smiled seductively as she held the bedroom door open.

'That's not what I meant,' Emmett said, pushing the door closed. 'I don't want to leave.'

'You misunderstood,' Allegra said. 'I'm not asking you to leave. I'm ending it. This relationship has reached its end date.'

She couldn't put herself in the path of any more pain. He was the first man she had trusted since Cole, but it all meant nothing in the end.

'We just had one fight,' Emmett said, taking her shoulders and trying to get her to look at him.

'No, we just told each other the truth.' She yanked away. 'I thought you were different. I thought you could see the real me, but you're just like the rest.'

All he could see was the slut, the party girl, the one who went from man to man. He didn't see who she truly was or what he meant to her, and he never would again. She might not have much, but she had her pride, and she wouldn't ever falter before another man.

She went to the bathroom and got dressed. When she opened the door, he wasn't in the

bedroom. Good, he'd left. She walked downstairs and found him waiting in the living room.

'I'm not leaving until we talk,' he said, looking
at her with pleading eyes.

'There's nothing to talk about.' She stalked to
the front door to throw it open when there was
a knock.

'Allegra,' a voice called out.

'Amethyst,' Allegra said, running to open the
door.

Amethyst stood on her doorstep, her eyes
red-rimmed.

'What's wrong?' Allegra asked.

Amethyst fell into her arms and began crying.
Allegra looked over her head at Emmett, feeling
panicked.

Chapter 16

Emmett watched as Allegra held Amethyst, comforting the teen as she cried as if her heart were breaking. When the worst wave of tears passed, Allegra gently lifted Amethyst to sit beside her. 'What happened?' She gently wiped her face with a tissue.

'She took the photo of you and my Mom. She said that it's not real. That you're lying, and she took it from me,' Amethyst cried.

Allegra looked at him, her gaze full of turmoil. Emmett had warned her that Imogen knew about the photo, but he hadn't imagined that it would come to this.

'But that's not right,' Amethyst asked, looking at Allegra with pleading eyes. 'You're not lying. You really knew my mother, didn't you?'

'Of course I'm not lying,' Allegra said, holding Amethyst's hands. 'Your mother and I knew each other. We were friends.'

Emmett knew Allegra was telling the truth, and he wondered how they were friends and why she was being evasive about that.

'Allegra, can I speak to you?' Emmett asked from behind the sofa.

Allegra nodded.

'I'll get you water,' Allegra said, rubbing Amethyst's back as she got up. 'Damn Imogen and her suspicions,' Allegra whispered when they entered the kitchen. 'I just wanted to see Amethyst once a week, get to know her, give Amy's daughter some much-needed comfort in her time of loss, but Imogen just refused to leave it be.'

'You need to call Imogen,' Emmett said.

Allegra tensed up at the mention of Imogen's name. 'I know Imogen needs to be notified where Allegra is, but I can't trust myself to talk to her now. You call her,' she said, getting a glass and filling it with water.

Emmett approached and took the glass from her hand, setting it on the counter. He put his hands on her shoulders and turned her to look at him. 'It would be better coming from you,' Emmett said. Imogen could call the police, which was the last thing that Allegra needed.

Allegra paused for a moment. 'I know what you're saying. I know this would be a good way of reassuring Imogen that her assumptions that I wanted to take Amethyst are wrong.' She sighed and leaned forward, laying her hand on Emmett's shoulder.

'Alright, I'll do it,' he said, weakening as he saw her vulnerability. It was the first time she'd leaned on him, and he realized he liked it. He enjoyed knowing that he was the one that she wanted to help her with her problems.

'Thank you.' She took the glass of water and returned to the living room.

Emmett took out his phone and dialed Imogen's number. He knew this was an important conversation and needed to handle it with care. He had to get Imogen to understand that Allegra only wanted Amethyst's best interests at heart and wasn't planning anything underhanded.

After a few rings, Imogen picked up, her voice tense as she answered, 'Hello?'

'Imogen, it's Emmett,' he began, his voice calm but serious. 'I wanted to let you know Amethyst is at Allegra's house right now. She's fine. They're talking, and it's probably best if—

She interrupted him, her words laced with anger. 'What is she doing there? I told her not to see Allegra again.'

'You know what she's doing here? She told us about the photo and your accusations.' Emmett fought to keep the frustration from his voice. He was frustrated with himself just as much as he was with her. He should have been more discreet.

'I'm coming.' Imogen hung up.

Damn it. He was supposed to stay calm and collected, and get Imogen on his side. Instead, he'd let his temper get the best of him.

Emmet returned to the living room, where Amethyst had calmed down and was sipping water, while Allegra had her arm around her shoulders.

'Your Aunt is coming,' Emmett said, trying to sound reassuring.

Amethyst looked at Allegra with fear. 'She's going to want me to go back, but I don't want to. Please, I want to stay with you just for tonight.'

Allegra hesitated, torn as she tried to decide what to do. Emmett quickly shook his head. He knew Allegra wanted to give Amethyst a safe place to work through her emotions, but Imogen was her guardian, and she had to return home with her.

'I don't know if I can do that,' Allegra said.

Amethyst nodded. She sat back on the couch as if the fight had gone out of her. 'Sometimes I feel like I'm invisible,' she murmured softly.

Allegra looked at him, distraught. He knew Imogen was not known for her diplomacy, but it seemed their relationship was much worse than he thought.

'I'll be right back,' she said and left for the kitchen, and Emmett quickly followed.

'Call Imogen,' she took the phone and handed it to him.

'Do you think this is a good idea?' Emmett asked, attempting to be the voice of reason.

'I can't let her do this. She's breaking Amethysts' spirit. Call her.'

Emmett nodded and dialed Imogen's number.

Allegra took the phone from him. 'Imogen, it's Allegra,' she said, cutting Imogen off mid-rant. 'Amethyst is staying here tonight. We'll come by tomorrow so she can get ready for school, and you and I will talk then.'

'No, I don't want that. I want her here tonight,' Imogen said, her voice full of frustration.

'She doesn't want to leave, and the only way you're going to get her back under your roof tonight is if you show up at my house with the police, and I promise you that if that happens, you will lose her forever,' Allegra snapped.

'I want to speak to Amethyst,' Imogen demanded, her voice curt.

'Fine.' Allegra carried the phone into the living room. 'It's your aunt,' she told Amethyst. 'I've told her you're going to stay the night, but she wants to talk to you.'

Amethyst shook her head. 'I don't want to talk to her.'

Allegra put the phone back to her ear.

'I heard,' Imogen snapped. 'You will not get away with this. I've hired a private investigator who is looking into your past as we speak. Once

I have proof about the gold-digger you truly are, I'll make sure you never see Amethyst again.'

'As always Imogen, it is a pleasure,' Allegra said as she hung up, her hand aching from how hard she was holding the receiver.

'What did she say?' Amethyst asked.

'You can stay here tonight. I'll take you home in the morning so you can get ready for school.'

Amethyst smiled with relief.

'I'll be right back,' Allegra said, forcing a smile.

'Was it really wise threatening her like that?' Emmett asked as he followed Allegra back to the kitchen.

'Oh, you don't have to worry about Imogen.' Allegra put the phone on the kitchen counter. 'She's apparently hired a private investigator to dig dirt on me.'

'That's just protocol,' Emmett said. 'It's not as if he'll find anything incriminating.'

Emmett knew Allegra had her reasons for keeping her past a secret, but he also wanted to ensure that there were no skeletons in her closet that could be used against her. 'Is there anything that the investigator could find?'

'No, of course not.' Allegra got a saucepan and poured milk into it.

Allegra hesitated, and Emmett could sense her inner turmoil. He wanted to help and be her confidant, but he also didn't want to push her too far.

'Because if there is anything, you can tell me, and I can help you.' Emmett stood behind her and put his hand on the counter beside her.

Allegra looked at him, her expression conflicted. She seemed torn between wanting to share her burdens and protecting her secrets.

'Help with what?' she asked, her voice tinged with vulnerability. She got three cups and lined them up on the counter.

'Help with Imogen, and with Virginia suing you. You're at risk legally, with both of them taking legal action.'

'Do you believe Virginia that I'm a gold-digger?' Allegra asked.

He hesitated, wanting to find a diplomatic way of telling her that evasiveness wasn't helping her cause.

'Of course you do. After all, you think I'm going to fall into bed with Mark.'

Allegra's reaction was swift and defensive. She stepped away from him, and Emmett immediately regretted bringing up the topic. He had no right to pry into her past, especially when she clearly wasn't ready to share.

'Of course I don't,' he quickly added, trying to reassure her. 'I'm asking you to tell me what's going on. I know that you're holding something back. Please, Allegra, let me in.' Emmett reached for her. 'I'm sorry about what I said about Mark. I was an idiot, a jealous idiot.'

He wanted to his head in a wall. He had let his past with Imogen come between them and tasted bitter regret that his own stupidity had driven this wedge between them.

She retreated further. Her voice wavered as she spoke. 'I can't deal with this tonight. I think you need to leave.'

Emmett sighed, realizing that pushing her any further would only cause more harm than good. 'Of course,' he said, his tone laced with regret. 'You have enough on your plate. We'll talk tomorrow.'

Emmett walked out of Allegra's house with a heavy heart. He had entered that evening intending to be there for her and Amethyst, but he couldn't help but feel like he had only made things worse. The tension between them, his jealousy, and now the revelation of Allegra's complicated past had all combined to create a rift between them.

As he got into his car and drove away from her house, he couldn't shake the feeling of regret. He had allowed his insecurities to get the best of him, and in doing so, he might have pushed Allegra further away. The thought that he might have ruined any chance of a future with her weighed on him like a heavy burden.

The drive back to his own home felt long and lonely. Emmett replayed the evening's events in his mind, each moment filled with missed opportunities and poorly chosen words. He had wanted to be there for Allegra, to support her, but he had added to her stress instead.

When he finally arrived at his house, he couldn't bring himself to go inside. Instead, he sat in his car for a while, staring at nothing in particular, lost in thought. He felt a sense of helplessness and frustration wash over him. How had he let his jealousy and insecurity drive a wedge between him and the woman he cared about?

Emmett knew he had to give Allegra space, to allow her the time she needed to sort through her own emotions and thoughts. But as he sat in his car, he couldn't help but fear that he had irreparably damaged their budding relationship.

Eventually, with a heavy sigh, he turned off the ignition and stepped out of the car. As he walked into his empty house, he couldn't shake the feeling of regret and missed opportunities. He hoped against hope that somehow, he could make amends and prove to Allegra that his feelings for her were genuine despite his earlier mistakes.

Chapter 17

Allegra nodded and watched him walk out. Even though on the surface, their fight had become background noise, she couldn't help but feel that everything had changed. She'd deliberately shut him out, and he knew it. How many times could she push him away and still expect him to come running back? She could have told him the truth about her parents, which would have reassured him, but she didn't want him to accept her by default. She wanted to know that he cared for her despite everything. He trusted her and believed she was a good person and worthy of his love, but right now, she felt like they were working at cross purposes.

The milk boiled, and Allegra returned the third cup to the cupboard. She had a guest she had to see to. She returned to the living room with a tray, carrying the hot cocoa and a plate of biscuits.

'I thought we could use this,' she said.

Amethyst nodded gratefully as she took the hot cup and sipped at it. 'My Aunt wants to stop you from seeing me ever again. She can't do that, can she?'

Allegra shook her head. 'I promise I will be here whenever you want me. Your Aunt cannot stop us from being friends.'

Amethyst smiled with relief. 'I knew you would stop her.' She looked around the room, her eyes settling on the flowers Emmett had brought the other night. 'I'm sorry I interrupted your date.'

'You didn't interrupt anything.' Allegra took a biscuit from the plate.

'Are you sure? Emmett seemed sad when he left.'

Allegra felt tears burn her eyes and rapidly blinked them back.

'Did you have a fight because of me?' Amethyst asked.

'No, of course not,' Allegra quickly reassured her. 'We were fighting before you arrived.'

'What about?'

'It's not important,' Allegra said.

Amethyst silently sipped her cocoa, her eyes wide with curiosity as she watched Allegra.

'It's grown-up stuff,' Allegra said, feeling the pull of her curiosity. 'Emmett was upset that Mark is my ex-boyfriend,' she finally said. 'He seems to think that if two people from the opposite sex are friends, then that automatically equals a relationship.

'Oh, that's understandable.'

'Why?' Allegra demanded. 'You can be friends with your ex.'

'Of course,' Amethyst said. 'It's just that Aunty Imogen was friends with Greg while she was engaged to Emmett.'

'Who's Greg?' Allegra asked.

'Her fiancé.'

Allegra felt her anger deflate. Oh, God, no wonder Emmett was so paranoid. His fiancé had stealth ambushed a breakup. He was probably paranoid that it would happen again. And instead of showing sympathy and giving him the chance to talk about it, she'd just broken up with him and shut him out.

'It's okay.' Amethyst reached out and clasped her hand. 'I'm sure it's not anything you can't talk about.'

Allegra smiled. She couldn't believe that this young girl was comforting her. 'I'm sure you're right.' She clasped her hand back. 'Do you want us to watch a movie?' Allegra asked, wanting to break the pall that hung over them. 'I've got Grease, and I haven't watched it in ages.'

Amethyst almost bounced off the couch in her excitement. As they watched the movie, Allegra was grateful for the distraction.

After they finished the movie, Allegra took Amethyst upstairs. 'You can sleep here tonight,' she said, taking her to the guest bedroom she'd refurbished with Joleen. The room was painted a pale green with a white wrought iron bed and a metal bedside table.

'This is beautiful,' Amethyst said, walking around the bedroom.

'I haven't finished it.' There were still some pieces she needed to buy, but it was at least decent enough for a guest.

'I'll get you my pajamas, and you can shower before bed.' When she returned, Amethyst was sitting on the bed with a smile on her face, looking around the room.

Allegra sat beside her on the bed and handed her the pajamas.

'Thank you for taking me in tonight,' Amethyst said. 'I wish...' She stopped herself from finishing the sentence and looked at Allegra shyly.

Allegra felt her heart speed up in anxiety. She knew Amethyst wanted her to ask her to finish the sentence, but if she did, she would open herself to further complications.

'I'd better let you sleep,' Allegra said, getting up briskly. 'If you need anything, just come to my room.'

Amethyst nodded. 'Good night, Allegra,' she said.

'Good night, Amethyst.' Allegra closed the bedroom door behind her with relief.

After she got ready for bed, she tossed and turned for hours. She finally fell asleep in the early hours of the morning. In her dream, she was in Imogen's house. Imogen was looking at her with displeasure. Allegra blinked, and suddenly she was in her mother's house. She climbed up the stairs to her bedroom. It was the same as when she'd left it when she was 14 to go to boarding school.

She opened the armoire and looked at the clothes she had lovingly recreated. The blazer twin set her mother had bought for her that she'd sewed rhinestones onto. The coat she changed the buttons on to add flair. The ribbon she'd carefully sewn on the outer hem of her pants. She took out the retro little black dress she'd bought at a garage sale and sat at her table where she'd set up her sewing supplies. Soon, she lost track of time as she carefully unstitched the dress so she could alter it to fit her.

Her mother came into her bedroom. She must have been calling her, but Allegra didn't hear her. Allegra looked up and saw the disappointment in her mother's face.

'Dinner is served,' her mother said and left.

Allegra dutifully hung the dress on a hanger and returned it to the armoire before she went down to dinner. The next day, she returned home from school and found her homemade clothes and the sewing kit she'd bought with her own savings gone. She'd felt like she'd been stabbed.

She got the diary she'd hidden in the floor-boards and wrote, 'I hate her. She wants me to be invisible. To cease to exist.'

Allegra woke up with a gasp. She hated those memories of her childhood and had done her best to eradicate them. As she lay with her arm over her head, she wondered why she'd dreamt about that day. She went to the closet where she had stacked the boxes she'd had in storage since leaving home. In one, she found her diaries. She searched the entries until she found the diary from when she was 13 and traced the words on the page. 'Oh God,' she whispered. It was as if an invisible connection was joining her and Amethyst together, and the more she tried to fight the bond, the more the universe tried to show her the truth.

She could see into the future. She could see the life that Amethyst was headed with her Aunt Imogen. The lack of care at home would make her search for a connection in other ways. In men, rather than herself. She realized in that moment when she'd told herself that she was happy with her life, and with her lack of connection, was a lie. She wanted more. She'd been so scared of getting hurt that she'd kept everyone at a distance. The only people who had truly entered her world were those she didn't have to worry about falling in love with: Maree, Joleen, Mark, Henry.

She needed to save Amethyst from the future that Allegra had lived, and to do that, she needed to see the one person she had avoided for eighteen years. Tomorrow, she needed to see her mother.

***

The next morning, Allegra drove Amethyst to Imogen's house. While Amethyst went upstairs to get ready for school, Imogen and Allegra talked downstairs.

Imogen was red-eyed and pale and had obviously had a hard night. 'I wish you had brought her home last night. Then she wouldn't be late for school, but I guess that's something only a parent would think about.'

Allegra sighed. How is it that Imogen could wrap up a complaint into a barb? 'She has plenty of time to get to school,' Allegra said. 'And I thought it was more important that she had some time and space.'

'You mean that you could turn her away from me.' Imogen clutched her cardigan tighter around herself and glared at Allegra.

'I don't need to do that. You're doing a good enough job yourself,' Allegra snapped. 'She told me you took the photo from her.'

'I'm going to prove it's a fake, and then your intrusions into our life will stop.'

'Didn't you think you should have had that conversation with me?' Allegra asked.

'Maybe you should have a conversation with *me* before giving her the photo.'

Allegra wanted to argue the point, but Imogen was right. If she had told her upfront about the photos and who she really was, things wouldn't have gotten so vicious. Although if Imogen hadn't been such a hard case, things would have been different, but Allegra kept that to herself.

'I'm sorry, you're right, I should have talked to you.' Allegra felt like the apology was choking in her throat.

Imogen looked nonplussed for a moment, and her eyes blinked rapidly in surprise.

'I just thought it would be a good memento of her mother,' Allegra said into the silence.

'It's a lie. You weren't friends with Amy. I knew Amy,' Imogen snapped, looking uncertain.

Allegra felt her anger burn. She'd apologized, but Imogen was like a dog with a bone. She wasn't about to let up. This was why she hadn't bothered talking to her in the first place.

'Did you know Amy when she was a child?' Allegra asked, her voice shaking with anger.

'I know that someone like her would never be friends with someone like you.' Imogen looked at Allegra as if she were looking at a turd on her shoe. 'I know what your plan is. You want to claim custody so you can control her money.'

Allegra wanted to rip Imogen to shreds with her tongue, but Amethyst began walking down the stairs, and she kept quiet.

'What are you talking about?' Amethyst asked, hearing the tail end of Imogen's accusation.

'I was just inviting you and your aunt over to dinner tonight. I wanted to prove to her I knew your mother.' Allegra shot Imogen a hard smile.

Imogen looked at her with uncertainty. 'Tonight?'

'We can go, can't we, Aunty Imi?' Amethyst asked.

'Of course we'll come,' Imogen said, putting her hand around Amethyst's shoulders. 'We'll see you tonight, Allegra.' She turned to Amethyst. 'Now let's get you to school.'

'See you later.' Allegra leaned forward and kissed Amethyst on the cheek.

Amethyst stepped away from Imogen and hugged Allegra. Allegra looked over her head and saw Imogen's eyes tearing up. She felt shaken. She had spent all this time angry at Imogen because she'd taken all her accusations personally and never actually thought about things from Imogen's point of view. Imogen had lost her brother and sister-in-law, and Amethyst was the only family she had left. She was attacking Allegra because she was afraid that she would lose her niece.

They walked out of the townhouse together. Amethyst got into Ruby and watched as Imogen led Amethyst to her car. Hopefully, her plan would ensure that they all got what they wanted. She started the ignition. Today was Wednesday, and if her mother followed the same routine she'd established while Allegra was growing up, she should be at the country club. Still, it was 17 years, and Allegra couldn't assume that her mother hadn't adopted some changes to her life. She called her mother's home number, and after a conversation with her housekeeper, she hung up, shaking her head. That woman followed her routine the same way that Big Ben's handles never stopped moving. Her mother had adopted golf as a young bride who wanted to impress her new husband, but within a few years, she had caught the bug and continued playing even after Allegra's father passed away.

When Allegra entered the club, it was like she never left. While they had redecorated it in the years she had been away, probably more than once, it had the same ambiance of hushed elegance. They established the club in 1897, and the clubhouse had classic heritage lines. It was one of the most exclusive country clubs in Los Angeles and frowned on celebrities. Hugh Hefner had once landed on the golf grounds because he was running late to a date with Katharine Hepburn and, after his airplane was towed and they presented him with the bill, had canceled his membership.

After chatting with reception, she found out that her mother was still on the green and settled in to wait in the restaurant. An hour later, she saw her mother walking off the green through the window and went to wait for her at the club entrance.

When Allegra approached, her mother didn't notice her until the woman opposite walking next to her spoke up. 'This must be your beautiful daughter, Adeline,' she said. 'She's the spitting image of you.'

Her mother turned around and looked at her, her face showing no surprise. Her mother was still beautiful at 73, and how she maintained her beauty was through regular Botox injections.

'My daughter has decided that we'll have tea here instead of at home,' her mother said, covering up the fact that they hadn't seen each other once in 17 years.

Adeline air kissed Allegra on the cheek and regally proceeded to the tearoom while Allegra followed. After they sat down, Adeline ordered high tea, and then she turned to Allegra and asked, 'What brings you here today?' as if she were talking to a passing acquaintance.

'I need your help.'

'Of course you do.' Her mother smiled smugly, and the saying 'like a cat that ate a canary' sprung into Allegra's mind.

Allegra swallowed, feeling as if shards of glass were lodged in her throat. She had vowed that she would never ask her mother for anything and wanted nothing more than to throw aside the high tea being served by a waiter and stomp off, never to see her mother again, but she couldn't. This wasn't just about her.

'I'm not here for me. I'm here for her.' She passed a photo to her mother. 'Her name is Amethyst.'

'I have a granddaughter,' her mother gasped as she lifted the photo to her face, her eyes softening as she noted the resemblance.

'She's not my daughter. She's Amy Revett's daughter,' Allegra said quickly before her mother had settled on the idea of a grandchild.

Her mother's eyes squinted slightly. She would have frowned if the skin on her forehead wasn't taut and immovable.

'I'm Amethyst's egg donor. I didn't see her at all growing up, but when Amy and David died, she tracked me down. She wants me to be involved in her life.'

'What on earth possessed you to donate an egg?' Her mother's voice was cutting and cold, her eyes even more so.

'I had my reasons,' Allegra said.

'If you want my help, then I deserve to know why?' her mother's voice was implacable. This was nothing that Allegra hadn't expected when she embarked on her mission of mercy, but it didn't make it any easier having to bow and scrape.

'I needed money, and I wanted to help Amy. It seemed like the perfect solution. I didn't know...' She wanted to finish the sentence that she didn't know she would feel such a bond with a child, but she didn't want to give her mother any more ammunition.

'Did you think a genetic bond was nothing?' her mother asked, finishing the sentence as if she had read Allegra's mind.

'I had no reason to believe otherwise,' Allegra said dryly.

Her mother's lips thinned, and she looked away. Allegra cursed herself for not holding back on her dig. She'd come here to get her mother's help, not spar with her.

Just when she was about to beg, her mother broke the silence and spoke. 'And what help do you need?'

'Her Aunt Imogen Revett thinks that I'm a gold-digger. That I'm only interested in being involved in Amethyst's life because I want her trust fund.'

'How absurd?' her mother took a sip of tea. Her family's trust fund made the Revett's look like paupers.

'But she won't believe me that I was friends with Amy or that I have no intention of trying to claim her.'

'You shouldn't have changed your name. Nobody would question a Wren,' her mother said, her eyes glittering with anger.

'That's why I changed my name,' Allegra said. She had always hated the way her mother wielded their family name like a weapon to get whatever she wanted, and her mother knew it.

Her mother let the silence stretch out as she took a leisurely sip of her tea. 'Your tea is getting cold, dear,' she said.

Allegra knew that her mother was signaling that they were being watched and that she had to act as if there was nothing untoward. Allegra poured herself a cup of tea and took a sip.

'Do you feel an attachment to the child?' Adeline asked, staring at Allegra's face as she waited for a response.

Allegra took a deep breath and met her mother's eyes head-on. Once she answered her mother's question and answered it truthfully, there would be no going back. She would give her mother power, and she knew from bitter experience Adeline had no trouble with abusing her position.

'Yes, I do.'

'Do you think that's wise? After all, she is not your progeny, and when you have your own, it could complicate the situation,' Adeline sounded almost maternal as she dispensed what she would have thought of as sound advice.

'I won't be having any progeny, so there are no issues of complications,' Allegra said.

'Those are a young woman's words,' Adeline said, waving her hand dismissively. 'You will change your mind.'

'No, I won't. I've never wanted children, and I never will.' Allegra felt like she was experiencing déja vu. When she was an adolescent, Adeline frequently told her that once she had her own children, she would know that the maternal decisions she was making were for Allegra's own good. When Allegra had told her she wouldn't be having children, Adeline had repeated the same sentence, word for word.

'Are you trying to punish me?' Adeline asked, her voice taking on a caustic edge.

'No, this has nothing to do with you,' Allegra said, feeling exasperated. 'I didn't want children then, and I don't want children now.'

Allegra waited, expecting Adeline to argue the point and try to sway her, but when she spoke again, her mother shocked her.

'When do I get to meet her?' she asked, tapping the photo of Amethyst on the table.

'You can meet her this afternoon. Come by my house at 4. I'll write the address.' Allegra opened her handbag and began rifling through for a pen and paper.

'There's no need,' Adeline said. 'I know your address.'

Allegra looked at her in confusion. She had never sent Adeline anything with her address, nor did they have any mutual friends.

'You didn't think I would let my daughter out into the world without keeping an eye on her, did you?' Adeline took another sip of tea.

Of course, her mother had kept tabs on her, probably via a private investigator.

'I am your mother, after all.' Adeline put down her cup on the saucer with a loud bang.

Allegra looked up in surprise. She noticed that her mother's hand was shaking. Adeline put her hand on her lap. Adeline's eyes were tearing, and her lip trembling slightly. Allegra had never seen her mother show such emotion.

'I'll be there tonight at 4,' Adeline said and stood. She walked past Allegra and out of the country club as regally as a queen. Allegra sat for a moment, not wanting to prolong their meeting by walking together to the entrance.

She had spent the past 17 years making her mother out to be a villain that she had to escape, but now she realized Adeline was just a woman, and an elderly woman at that. When she had decided on this meeting, she had imagined all kinds of scenarios that involved her complete and utter humiliation. She had never for a moment imagined that her mother would help her without a murmur of protest or that she would get emotional about seeing her only daughter.

Perhaps her mother was softening, or maybe Allegra herself was learning to see her mother through a more objective lens and not one colored by adolescent rebellion. While Adeline had never been maternal, nor had she been a good mother to Allegra, perhaps she had loved her in her own way and shown it the best way she could.

Chapter 18

Emmett sullenly drank his morning coffee, wearing regret after his fight with Allegra like a bad cologne.

Rhys buttered his toast and sat down, taking a bite, the crunch echoing in the too-quiet kitchen. As Emmett played with his eggs, Rhys cocked his head. 'Why aren't you eating?'

'I'm not hungry.' Emmett pushed his plate away and took a sip of coffee.

'You don't eat if there's something wrong,' Rhys proclaimed.

Emmett internally sighed. He should have known better than to let Rhys notice his morose mood. 'Allegra and I had a fight last night, but it will be okay.'

Rhys took another bite of toast.

As Emmett was putting their dishes in the dishwasher, the doorbell rang. He went to open the door, feeling a surge of hope that it was Allegra. He opened it with a smile, only to frown as he saw Imogen on the other side. Her hair was disheveled, and her usual perfect demeanor slightly askew.

'I need your help,' she pleaded, her hand clutching his arm.

He shook her off, anger surging through him. It was her fault he'd fought with Allegra last night. She was the source of his insecurity, the one who had made him look at Mark as a potential love rival, not to mention that his indiscretion in revealing the photo of Amethyst and Amy had brought about their whole stupid fight.

'I have nothing for you.' He placed his hand on the other side of the door frame, preventing her from coming in.

'Please, Emmett. Allegra is going to take Amethyst away from me. It's not right. I'm her aunt. I love her.'

He wanted to slam the door in her face, but he couldn't be that cruel. She was genuinely terrified that Allegra would take custody of Amethyst. 'Allegra only wants to know Amethyst. Be there for her. It's your own insecurity that's pushing Amethyst more toward her.' He cursed himself as he said the words, realizing that's exactly what he had done. His own insecurity had probably pushed Allegra into Mark's arms. An image of the two of them together flashed behind his retina, and he quickly pushed it away. He needed to stop with this jealousy and trust Allegra.

He stepped away from Imogen, needing a breath, and she took advantage, following him into the apartment and closing the door behind her.

'Is that true? She really doesn't want custody?'

Her plaintive voice caught him off guard, and he turned to look at her. Tears were seeping down her face as she desperately bit her lip, trying to hide them.

'Yes, it is.' He went to the side table next to the couch, got a tissue box, and handed it to her. 'You need to give Allegra a chance and stop thinking the worst.' And he needed to take the same advice and stop his crazy jealousy.

Imogen got a tissue and wiped her face, collecting herself.

'That's the first time I've seen you cry,' he murmured. He'd known her for so many years, and she'd never appeared out of control or vulnerable. She had always maintained her perfect veneer and control.

'I know.' She smiled ruefully. 'I wanted to be the perfect girlfriend and the perfect fiancé for you, and that meant never showing any vulnerability.'

She held his gaze, and he realized the moment was charged. Rhys barged in, his backpack on his back, and he was thankful he broke the tension.

Rhys looked between them meaningfully. 'Are you two getting back together because you and Allegra fought?'

Emmett cursed himself as he saw Imogen's face brighten. 'No, Allegra and I are still together. Imogen and I are talking.'

'Okay. See you later,' Rhys said, heading for the door to catch a bus to his chess club.

'So you and Allegra fought?' Imogen asked after Rhys left.

'That's private,' he snapped, irritated by her cheerfulness.

'I know. I know. You don't owe me anything. I'm sorry.' Imogen placed the tissue box back on the side table and sat on the sofa.

He cursed again. He wanted to end this conversation, not prolong it.

'I'm so sorry about the way things ended with us.' Imogen turned to look at him, her blue eyes full of contrition. 'I want you to know I never cheated with you on Greg. I broke off our engagement before we embarked on a relationship.'

He knew he shouldn't care. After all, it was old history and completely irrelevant, but he couldn't help but feel relieved. There was no worse feeling than being a cuckold, and he was glad to know the truth.

'I got so caught up in the emotion of it all. Our relationship was so controlled. So predictable.' She frowned at her hands.

He couldn't help but be intrigued by the turn the conversation was taking and sat on the sofa next to her. He'd never had closure about their relationship. He had been living what he thought was the perfect life, with his future beckoning one day, and the next, he was a single man responsible for a teenager with special needs.

'I liked our life,' he said.

'So did I.' She reached for him, holding his forearm. 'I was so happy. You were the man I'd always dreamed about marrying, but when Rhys came into the picture, I couldn't deal with the unpredictability and messiness of it all. I was ill-prepared and immature, and I fell for Greg for all the wrong reasons.' She sighed. 'I had a future mapped out of our two children and the house already picked out.'

'I remember,' he said. They'd had so many conversations planning their lives. Picking out the schools their children would go to and what area they wanted to live in. Having the perfect family life he'd grown up with.

'I took you for granted. I didn't appreciate what a wonderful husband and father you could be.' She looked at him with longing in her eyes.

He knew she was imagining their future now. They both had adolescents to care for, and they could still have their own family, not the three children they had intended, but perhaps one or two. And perhaps in a few years' time, when Rhys and Amethyst were in college and moving on with their lives. As he saw them in their perfect house together, planning dinner parties with people just like them, he realized that wasn't the future he wanted anymore. He didn't want the regular tedium of the suburbs. He didn't want any children.

He wanted Allegra. When he saw his future with her, they were living in the mansion together. She was running ballroom classes while he had a home office where he ran his private practice. It was a life full of vibrant passion and color, of laughter and joy.

He came back to the present to find Imogen leaning in. 'We could still have all that. We could be together.'

Emmett took her hand off his arm. 'No, we can't. I love Allegra. She's the woman I want to spend the rest of my life with.'

Imogen's face darkened with disappointment, and she opened her mouth to say something more, but she must have seen the resolution on his face, for she quickly pursed her lips closed and nodded.

He stood and gestured toward the door. She followed him slowly.

'You know that she's not what she says she is?' Imogen said. 'I hired a private investigator, and he found she changed her name when she was 19.'

'I know everything I need to know about her,' Emmett said firmly.

Imogen let out a long sigh. He opened the door for her and watched her walk out. She quickly turned before he closed the door. 'I hope she's everything you think she is.'

'She is,' he said firmly, closing the door on her.

Now, he had to get Allegra back. His phone pinged that there was an SMS, and he saw it was a message from Allegra, inviting him over for a dance mixer. He smiled joyfully. His prayers were being answered.

Chapter 19

Allegra finished arranging flowers on the side table and stepped back to look at her living room. She had spent the afternoon cleaning and arranging all her knick-knacks. She felt strangely nervous about hosting her mother. During the day, it had dawned on her that her mother had never been a guest in her house. Allegra had been her mother's dependent, and then she'd cut all ties. There had been no opportunity to transition through the different stages of adulthood and experience the gradual release that usually marked parental relationships. Now, her mother was coming to her house to help her, and Allegra felt like her whole world felt slightly off-kilter.

There was a knock on the door. Allegra looked at her watch. It was 3.50. Could her mother really be early? She doubted it. Her mother was always punctual. While she viewed lateness as slovenly, she also viewed being early as in poor taste, making her chauffeur idle slowly toward the house to arrive exactly at the appointed time. Allegra sighed as she realized who it was.

'You're early,' Allegra said as she opened the front door.

'Is that a problem?' Imogen asked.

'No, of course not.' Allegra forced a smile as Amethyst peered over Imogen's shoulder, her smile bright enough to power a nuclear plant. Allegra let Imogen through and gave Amethyst a quick hug and a kiss. 'You look lovely.' Amethyst was wearing a vintage 1930s Good Fortune dress Allegra had given her as a present. The dark blue rayon and lace collar highlighted her face. She'd even attempted a matching hairstyle and had pinned her hair. 'I was right. It suits you much better.' Allegra had planned on altering it for herself, but when Amethyst had seen it on her dressmaker dummy, she had fallen in love with it, so Allegra had asked her to try it on, and it fit perfectly.

'Would you like some cheese and crackers?' Allegra asked once her guests were seated. 'I was just about to bring it in.'

'No, I'm not interested in anything from you except for the truth,' Imogen said haughtily. Catching sight of Amethyst's sad face, Imogen forced a smile. 'I'm sorry, I'm just dying of curiosity to hear about your news.'

'All in good time,' Allegra said, forcing herself to smile pleasantly in return. 'And what about you, Amethyst?'

Amethyst looked from her aunt to Allegra and finally nodded shyly.

'I'll be back in a moment,' Allegra said. 'Please make yourself comfortable.'

Allegra walked into the kitchen and grabbed hold of the kitchen counter. She had to stop letting Imogen push her buttons. Allegra counted to 60 before picking up the cheese tray. She just had to stall for ten minutes until her mother arrived and created a safe buffer while Allegra dropped her bombshell.

'Here we go,' Allegra said as she returned to the living room and placed the cheese and crackers on the table. 'How was school today?' Allegra asked Amethyst.

'Great.'

Damn teenagers and their monosyllabic responses. 'How did you go with the science project you were doing with Rhys?' Allegra asked, hoping for a longer response.

'We got an A.' Amethyst took a bite of watercress cracker smeared with Brie.

Well, she was going to be of no more help.

'So, how did you know Amy?' Imogen asked.

'Our families knew each other very well.' Allegra picked up a cheese skewer and put it in her mouth. 'Our fathers were best friends, and that put us in each other's path throughout my childhood,' she said when she finished chewing. 'Growing up, Amy even babysat me.'

'Amy had no friends named Kenton.' Imogen was in full-on cross-examination mode. Her face was calm, and only the strain in her voice betrayed her rising emotion.

'That's because Kenton isn't my actual name. I changed it when I was 18 years old from Wren,' Allegra said. She hated talking about this part of her life, and there were only three people she had shared the truth with in the past, Maree, Henry, and Joleen.

'Are you claiming that you're a descendant of the Wrens?' Imogen's voice was full of disbelief.

'That's right.'

'That's preposterous. I know Adeline Wren, and she has no daughter.' Imogen looked at Amethyst and smiled. 'Besides which, who in their right name would change their name if they were a Wren?'

Amethyst was looking from her aunt to Allegra in confusion.

'Someone who doesn't care about names and privilege and lineage. Someone who believes that people should be taken for what they are.' Allegra was fighting for calm, but her voice was going up as she talked.

'I don't believe a word of this,' Imogen snapped. 'We're leaving.' She took Amethyst's hand as she stood and yanked her off the sofa. Amethyst stood, her eyes wide with fear.

There was a knock on the door. Allegra sighed in relief. She glanced at her watch. It was 3.59. The old lady was showing her eagerness.

'You don't have to believe me,' Allegra said as she stood. 'You can ask my guest.' She walked to the front door and opened it. Adeline gave her an air kiss as she passed.

'I believe you know my mother, Adeline Wren,' Allegra said when she returned to the living room.

Imogen was staring at Adeline in shock. Allegra performed the introductions, and Adeline nodded at Imogen before walking past her to Amethyst with her hands stretched out. 'Let me look at you dear,' she said as she took Amethyst's hands in her own. 'Yes, you're the picture of what Allegra was like at your age.'

As Adeline sat down, she pulled Amethyst to sit down beside her on the couch. 'You sit here, my dear. So I can look at you properly.'

Imogen sat down, her eyes darting from Adeline to Allegra to Amethyst. The resemblance was striking. It was as if they were on the set of a science fiction show and were looking through a time portal that showed one character at three stages of their life: teenager, woman, and senior.

'I brought you a little gift,' Adeline said as she handed Amethyst a gift bag. 'I have had little contact with young people these days, so I had to ask a friend for help. I hope it is to your taste. She assured me that young people these days love it.'

Amethyst opened the bag and took a boxed set of the Divergent series. 'Thank you, Mrs Wren.' Amethyst smiled as she saw the books.

'Please, don't be so formal, dear. After all, we are family.' Adeline looked at Imogen as she made her point. 'Your dear mother was like a second daughter to me, and your grandmother was my best friend. Why don't you call me Gamma?'

'I don't think that's suitable,' Imogen piped up. 'You're not her grandmother.'

'And why not?' Adeline looked at her with a lifted eyebrow. 'After all, that's what Allegra called Nellie, Amy's mother. You see, the Wrens and the Finchs have been friends since we were young. We were each other's flock, and you know what flocks of the same feather do, don't you?'

As her mother talked, Imogen sank back into the couch, looking defeated. Allegra had wanted to shut Imogen up and stop her constant suspicion and accusations, not break the woman.

'Mother, I'm going to get tea. Would you like to help me, Imogen?' Allegra asked.

Imogen looked at her blankly for a moment before her face cleared, and she nodded. 'Of course,' she said, slowly following Allegra to the kitchen.

Allegra started the kettle, trying to decide how to start a conversation, but she was drawing a blank. Anything she said at this point could be construed as a victory dance. Allegra glanced over at Imogen, who had her arms wrapped around her waist as she stared out of the window.

'I'm not stupid,' Imogen said, noticing her glance. 'I know that I have no chance against the Wren millions. You'll file a suit, and once your mother does her testimonial, you'll get custody.'

'I don't want custody,' Allegra said.

'What do you mean?' Imogen looked at her in confusion. 'That's what you always wanted.'

'No, what I wanted was for Amethyst to have a sense of her identity. I give her that, and so does my mother, but you are her aunt. You are her blood. You were the one that her mother and father appointed as a guardian.'

'You don't want me,' Amethyst said, entering the kitchen. She was looking at Allegra with wounded eyes.

'No, that's not what I'm saying.' Allegra walked over and put her hands on her shoulders. 'I'm saying I want a relationship with you and to see you regularly. For us to be a part of each other's lives, but your aunt is your guardian.' She turned toward Imogen. 'She is the one who has the family history, who knows about you and your parents. I'm a link in the chain, and I'm going to be there for you, always.'

Amethyst smiled. 'But I want to see you more than just sometimes at school.'

Imogen came closer and put her hand on Amethyst's shoulder. 'We can probably look at arranging a regular visitation schedule.'

'And sleepovers.' Amethyst looked at her aunt pleadingly.

'We can work up to that,' Imogen said.

It surprised Allegra that Imogen capitulated. The tension lines were gone from her face, and Imogen looked at peace.

'Now that we've resolved that, let's have some tea.' Allegra carried the tray.

'I'll get the cakes,' Imogen said, lifting the cake stand and following her into the living room.

Allegra served tea and watched her guests interact with each other. Now that Imogen re-alized she had nothing to fear from Allegra, it was like a mask had come down. She displayed a tenderness toward her niece that Allegra had never seen before. How could she have thought that Imogen didn't love her niece? Imogen had spent the past month in a panic at the thought that she would lose Amethyst. Perhaps fear did strange things to a person and put their worst qualities on display.

Adeline asked Amethyst and Imogen questions, settling into the role of benevolent grandmother, while Allegra looked around in surprise at how her makeshift family had become so big and complicated. She should have felt over the moon that her plan had worked, but instead, she felt slightly deflated. She kept thinking about Emmett and wondering where he was and what he was doing.

After Allegra walked Imogen and Amethyst out, she returned and found her mother examining the living room.

'You've done well for yourself,' Adeline said.

'Thank you.' Allegra stood by the couch, uncertain about what to do. 'And thank you for coming. If it hadn't been for you, I wouldn't have been able to get through to Imogen.'

'It's the least I could do,' Adeline said dryly. 'I've also spoken to our lawyers, and they will release your trust fund by the end of the week.'

'You didn't have to do that,' Allegra said. Her 36th birthday was still three months away.

'I know, but I want to.' Adeline suddenly looked tired, and she sat on the sofa. 'I want to be in your life, and I want nothing to come between us anymore.'

Her mother had attempted to use her trust fund to bring her back in line when she was younger, but Allegra had refused to buckle to the pressure and had stubbornly made her own way in the world. 'I wish you'd realized this 17 years ago,' she said, bitterness rising within her.

'We all make mistakes.' Adeline hesitated, looking uncharacteristically uncertain, as if she were trying to think through what she wanted to say. 'I wanted to come and see you last year,' she finally said, 'when you were being treated for your cancer.'

Allegra blinked. 'How did you know about my diagnosis?'

'I've had a private investigator keep regular tabs on you to make sure you would be all right,' Adeline said. 'I came and saw Henry, and we spoke a few times. He was the one who advised that I wait until you had recovered before I approached you.'

Allegra wasn't surprised that Henry had met her mother and not told her about it. He was a true old-world gentleman who believed in maintaining confidences, which was why she had trusted him with all her secrets.

'So why didn't you?' Allegra asked.

Adeline said nothing, just sat there looking like an old woman. Allegra wanted to be angry with her mother for not reaching out and taking the first step to heal the rift, but she had to take stock. While her mother's pride may have stood in the way then, she had stepped up when Allegra asked.

'It doesn't matter,' Allegra said. 'The past is the past. All we can do is focus on the future.'

Adeline smiled slightly. 'You have changed,' she said.

Allegra felt a lightness as she realized it was true. She had changed. She didn't want to dwell on past transgressions. Instead, she wanted to look forward to the future. While she and her mother would never be close, too much had passed for that. They could at least be on the fringes of each other's lives.

'Yes, I have,' Allegra acknowledged.

'I'm glad,' Adeline said. 'And now I should get going.'

Allegra walked her mother out.

Henry came to her again that night. She was in the ballroom wearing a 1950s full-skirt party dress, with a white silk underdress covered with a black lace overskirt. Henry was in the corner waiting for her, wearing the Zoot suit he'd died in.

'There you are, toots,' he said, walking over and taking her into his arms. A band appeared in the corner and started playing.

'That's new.' Allegra nodded at the band as she came out of a spin and back into his arms.

'Some musician fellas wanted to start a band, so I thought I'd give them something to play for.

Plus, it gives me the chance to put this suit to use.'

They danced in silence for a few moments, the fast jazz song making them jive and bop. The music changed, the band started playing a slow, mournful song, and Allegra and Henry transitioned into a slow dance.

'You didn't tell me you'd met my mother,' Allegra said, lifting her head from Henry's shoulder.

'I figured the two of you would work out your troubles when the time was right.' Henry dipped her and brought her back up. 'And I was right.'

'Is that a ghost thing?' Allegra asked. 'You have the gift of seeing the future.'

'I don't need to see the future to tell you that you need to do something about that young man of yours.'

Allegra missed a step and trod on Henry's foot.

'A man will only take so much punishment, and you've reached that limit.'

He wasn't saying anything that she didn't already know, but it didn't mean that she liked hearing it.

'So what are you going to do?' he asked.

'Nothing. There's nothing to do.'

Suddenly, the band disappeared and they stopped dancing.

Henry shook his head sadly. 'You're blowing it.'

Henry disappeared, and she was all alone on the dance floor. The ballroom got darker, and she was standing in a spotlight and couldn't see anything around her but darkness.

She shouted Henry's name. 'Come back,' she screamed until her throat was raw, but she remained alone.

Allegra woke up with a gasp, her heart thumping with fear. She sat up in bed and smelled aftershave.

'You are an evil man, Henry,' she said. He'd given her the cliched revelatory ghost experience, trying to inspire fear so that she would stop lying to herself. She heard his laughter on the breeze. 'Okay, you win.'

As she lay back and closed her eyes, she felt him kiss her gently on the cheek. 'That's my girl,' he whispered, leaving her to dream.

Chapter 20

Emmett heard the music as he got out of his car, its lively notes resonating through the cool night air. It sounded like a party was in full swing, the rhythmic beats of a jazz tune setting the mood. He made his way to the grand entrance of the mansion, ready to knock on the door, but before he could even lift his hand, the door swung open, revealing a world of music and laughter inside.

'Hello?' Emmett called out as he stepped into the elegant foyer. His voice echoed through the empty space, met only by the distant strains of jazz music. He had received a text from Allegra inviting him to her place for a gathering with friends. It was an olive branch he had eagerly accepted. He hated how things ended last time and wanted to talk things through.

Emmett followed the enchanting melodies through the opulent mansion, guided by the faint laughter and clinking glasses. It didn't take long for him to find the source of the mu-sic—a grand ballroom filled with dancing couples, twirling and swaying to the rhythm of the jazz band. The sight that greeted him stole his breath away.

In the center of the ballroom, Allegra was a vision. She wore a navy and white polka dot swing jive dress that accentuated her every curve, the bodice snug around her waist while the full skirt swayed with her every movement. Her dancing partner was Mark, and together they moved in perfect harmony with the music, their steps intricate and their chemistry undeniable. The room was alive with energy, yet it felt like time had slowed down for Emmett, and Allegra was the only person in focus.

Watching her, Emmett was transported back to the first time he had seen her dance at the club, her face radiating joy and life. He had once been jealous of seeing her in Mark's arms, but now all he felt was an overwhelming sense of pride. They were a perfect match, and while the other dancers in the room were talented, their eyes couldn't help but drift toward Allegra and Mark, drawn to the magnetic presence they exuded.

Emmett realized he had been such a fool, letting his jealousy and insecurities get the better of him. He hadn't listened to Allegra when she had tried to explain how much dancing meant to her. But now, as he watched her dance, he understood. He had to find a way to make things right, prove to her that he was willing to change, grow, and support her in pursuing her passions.

An African American man wearing a white Zoot suit, and black shirt, with a heavy chain hanging off his belt, approached him. He offered his hand with a friendly smile. 'Emmett.'

'I'm sorry. Have we met?' Emmett asked as they shook hands.

'Yes, we have honey,' the man said in a higher-pitched voice.

Emmett felt his jaw drop. 'Joleen,' he said, noticing that the man had Joleen's height. He looked closer and recognized Joleen's face without makeup and false eyelashes.

'Joe now,' Joe said in a deep voice.

A little boy of about six years of age appeared beside him, dressed in an identical suit. He looked like a little mini Joe. 'This is my son, Lucas, and this is my friend, Emmett,' Joe told Lucas.

Emmett shook the tiny hand offered to him. Lucas moved away to the full-length mirror and danced, replicating Michael Jackson's moonwalk as he watched himself.

Emmett turned back to Joe, his curiosity piqued. 'I didn't recognize you,' he admitted.

'You're not supposed to,' Joe said. 'My ex only lets me see my son if I'm Joe. When I'm not with him, I can be the real me.'

Emmett nodded, trying to understand what kind of life Joe was living. Joleen was the real him, while Joe was the impostor. Wouldn't it be much easier to just live as Joe and have Joleen as an occasional dress-up?

'I couldn't be Joe anymore,' Joe said, as if he'd read Emmett's mind. He lifted the cuff of his shirt, and Emmett saw his scars. 'At least now I get to be who I am inside.' Joe carefully pulled down his cuffs.

'Have you thought about having an operation?' Emmett asked, wondering why Joleen didn't become a permanent citizen.

Joe nodded, a wistful look in his eyes. 'Thought about it, dreamed about it, dying for it, but I can't do it. Not until Lucas is older.' He watched Lucas with pain in his eyes. 'A young boy needs his father, even if his father is a flaming queen.' Joe smiled wryly as he put a Joleen inflection in his voice.

They stood in silence, and Emmett's eyes turned back to Allegra. He caught her glancing at him, but she glanced away and turned back to her dance partner.

'She's like me too,' Joe said suddenly, his gaze shifting to Allegra, who was still dancing in the center of the ballroom. 'The broken can recognize each other. She thinks that she's broken inside and that all she's worth is some lust between the bedsheets. If you want her, you'll have to prove to her she is more.'

Emmett nodded, his gaze never leaving Allegra. 'She's kind and loyal and full of fire. She makes me feel alive in a way I've never felt before.'

Joe placed a comforting hand on Emmett's shoulder. 'It's not me you have to tell. Convince her.'

Emmett had been tracking Allegra's movements throughout the ballroom, but every time he got close, she gracefully moved away. He patiently waited for a slow song, knowing this was his chance. When the music changed to a melodic tune, he strode to the middle of the dance floor and gently tapped Mark on the shoulder. 'I believe this is my dance,' Emmett said with a confident smile, offering his hand to Allegra.

Mark hesitated for a moment, surprise in his eyes, but before he could object, Emmett had already taken Allegra into his arms and swept her onto the dance floor. They swayed to the slow rhythm, their bodies naturally fitting together. He couldn't believe that he'd spent his adolescence cursing his old-fashioned grandmother's insistence that he spend time learning ballroom dancing, and finally, in this moment, when he needed to make a romantic gesture, he could.

Allegra's eyes widened as he led her into a foxtrot.

'This is a surprise,' Allegra said, her voice a soft murmur, her body effortlessly melting into his.

Emmett chuckled softly. 'Me being here or being able to dance?'

'Both,' Allegra said. 'I didn't think you would come, not after our last conversation.'

'I'm harder to shake off than you think.' Emmett led her gracefully across the dance floor, his gaze never leaving hers.

Allegra's eyes held a mixture of curiosity and something else, something Emmett couldn't quite decipher. 'So you did get the message that I'm trying to shake you off?'

'You'll have to try harder.' Emmett swung her out and brought her back. 'Because I'm sticking.'

Allegra appeared to want to say more, but then her gaze shifted to something—or someone—over Emmett's shoulder. He followed her line of sight, turning to see a striking couple making their entrance. The woman wore a shimmering golden gown that radiated elegance, while the man beside her donned a classic tuxedo. Emmett blinked as he recognized the bright blue eyes and strong jaw of Tom Calvert, the movie star.

'Maree,' Allegra gasped, her eyes lighting up, and she hurriedly made her way to the couple. They embraced, and Emmett followed.

'This is my best friend, Maree,' Allegra introduced them. 'And her husband Tom.' She embraced him while Emmett shook hands with Maree and then Tom.

'It looks beautiful,' Maree remarked, her gaze sweeping across the grand ballroom. 'I can't wait to see the old dame when you've renovated.'

'Me too,' Allegra replied, her eyes gleaming with excitement as she glanced around the ballroom.

They returned to the dance floor. 'You've got famous friends,' Emmett remarked, smiling as they swayed to the music.

'That's from when I was a costume designer on the soapie,' Allegra explained.

Mark appeared at his side. 'It's time,' he told Allegra.

Allegra nodded. 'We're doing our performance piece,' she told Emmett.

'Can't wait to see it. Thanks for letting me cut in,' Emmett said, offering his hand to Mark.

Mark smiled in response as they shook hands, and Allegra watched Emmett with a perplexed look, clearly conflicted by the emotions swirling within her.

Chapter 21

Allegra watched him walk away and felt her knees go weak. She thought she'd pushed him away once and for all and that he wouldn't come back for more punishment. She'd sent the text as a safe option and arranged that they meet at the social mixer for their dance school, giving her a safe buffer. Even though he'd confirmed he was coming, when he arrived, she hadn't known what to do, so she did what she did best, nothing. She ignored him, wondering if he would go away.

Mark nodded for the music to start, and Joe flicked on the new track. She fell into dancing with Mark on automatic pilot, her mind still on Emmett. When she stumbled on a step and caught Mark's annoyed face, she got her head into the game and concentrated. When they finished, she sought Emmett and found him watching her as he clapped wildly, a proud smile on his face.

Joe turned the music back on, and the dancers drifted back to the dance floor. A female dancer, one of her regulars from Tuesday's class, asked Emmett to dance.

Joe came over and stood with her. 'He'll only keep trying so many times if you freeze him out.'

Allegra looked at him with sorrow. 'I don't know what to do.' When she'd invited Emmett, it seemed obvious that they needed to talk and get everything out, but now she was scared that it would just be too hard once they did. 'We've said some terrible things to each other, and I don't know if we can come back from that.' She was still smarting that he couldn't trust her not to sleep with Mark.

'Don't sell yourself short, and most important-ly, don't sell him short. He's here. He's still trying.'

'But should it be this much work?'

'You're the one who's making it hard work. You've been keeping him at arm's length, and you're still holding back.' Joe took her arm and held her. 'We're both alike. We got a second chance.' He ran his hand over his scarred wrist. 'The problem is you're wasting yours.'

Allegra bit her lip and finally nodded.

'That's my girl.' Joe turned her toward Emmett and gently pushed her toward him. 'Go get your man.'

Allegra walked over. Emmett finished his dance and turned to her. Stepping into his arms was the most natural thing in the world.

'We need to talk,' she said, looking up at him.

'Yes, we do. But not now.' He put his hand on her back and pulled her closer to him.

Allegra closed her eyes as she rested her head on his shoulder. They danced the rest of the track in silence. While she danced, she couldn't stop thinking about Joe's advice. Emmett was here, even after everything. Wasn't it time she just stopped putting up barriers and let things happen? After they finished, she attempted to mingle with the rest of her guests, and Emmett accepted every dance invitation.

Hours later, she walked the last of the guests out. When she returned, Emmett was standing in the middle of the ballroom.

'Watching you tonight, I realized something.' He turned to look at her. 'Dancing is more than just a recreational activity. It's where you feel alive. I'm sorry about the way I reacted about Mark. I was a jealous idiot.'

Allegra was flabbergasted. He was saying everything she dreamed about him saying, yet she didn't feel the joy she should feel.

'Do you forgive me?' he asked.

'Why did you react that way?' she asked.

He looked away, as if he was embarrassed. 'You know the story about Imogen. Well, what I didn't tell you is that she got engaged to Greg a month after we broke up, and he was her client for six months before that.'

'Do you think she cheated on you?' Allegra asked.

'I never asked.' He looked back at her. 'You didn't answer my question.'

'I know.' Allegra stepped away and clenched her hands together. 'It's not a question of me forgiving you. It's a question of you forgiving me. I haven't been completely honest with you.'

Allegra felt her stomach cramping with nervousness. She didn't think she would feel like this, but now that the moment of truth was here, she realized she was terrified that Emmett wouldn't forgive her for being so secretive. And if he didn't, then where would she be? She realized she loved him, only now that she was facing the moment of possibly losing him forever.

'You see, I'm not really Allegra Kenton. I changed my name when I was 18 so no one would know where I truly came from. My birth name is Allegra Wren. My parents are John and Adeline Wren.'

She finally glanced over at Emmett.

'When you accused me of holding something back, this was it. I didn't want you to know about where I came from.'

'Did you think I would care? That I would pursue you for your money?' Emmett asked, his face darkening with anger.

'I don't know. I just wanted to know that you wanted me for me, and no other reason.' Allegra knew she should get closer to him to try to make physical contact, but something held her back.

'I never cared about money or where you come from. I only wanted you. I love you.'

Allegra started crying. This was what she was terrified of hearing. She feared caring too much. Of making herself vulnerable.

'What's wrong?' Emmett hugged her as she cried, her hands grasping his shirt as sobs tore through her body.

'I love you too,' Allegra whispered, her body shaking.

'Then what's the problem?' Emmett tucked her hair behind her ears and used his handkerchief to wipe her face.

'I'm scared. Whenever I love people, they either leave or die.'

'I'm here, and I'm staying.' Emmett looked into her eyes, and she knew she could believe him. He was the real thing. He always was, and that's why she fought her feelings for so long.

She tilted her head and kissed him. She thought she had done many dangerous things before, but her biggest adventure yet would be falling in love and being loved in return.

***

Dreams of Destiny Series

Dreams of Destiny series are suspense novels featuring lovers searching for a dream, when love finds them at the most inconvenient time. They feature secret identities, hidden agendas and thwarted ambition.

You've already met Tom and Maree in the first book of the series. Book 2 features Maree's best friend, Allegra, and Book 3 is about Gerald 'Mack' Mackevoy as we discover what he's doing impersonating a homeless person.

Hollywood Dreams

She's fallen for his greatest role. But can she fall for him?

Vintage Dreams

She had to nearly die before she could live again. Can she build a new life on the embers of her old one?

Vengeful Dreams

She's dreamed of vengeance since she was a young girl. Can she find redemption in love?

For more information go to

https://www.amrapajalic.com/dreams-of-destiny-romance-series.html

Hollywood Dreams

She's fallen for his greatest role. But can she fall for him?

Former soap star Tom Calvert dreams of making movies that matter. To get the part of a lifetime, he becomes a method actor, living as Beau Tennant, a war hero with a disabling injury. While in character, he meets Maree Reynard, a costume designer, and takes her on a date. But when this practice date becomes all too real, he realizes that he's made the mistake of a lifetime. Will he be able to get Maree to fall in love with Tom Calvert?

Maree Reynard's father is an actor, and she has grown up on a studio lot. She has no illusions about the artifice of the movie-making business and has vowed she would never date an actor. When she meets and falls in love with Beau Tennant, she knows that she's found her dream man who is genuine and real. But when Beau disappears from her life, she is heartbroken. She meets Tom Calvert on the rebound and sees their flirtation as a way of recovering her shattered confidence. Will Tom Calvert be able to convince her he is the real deal?

Return to Me

A fatal accident. A parallel world. Second chances don't come often.

Death has never been far from Lana. In a previous life, her husband Frank died from a heart condition at thirty. In this new world where she's known as Alannah Walker, it's Tristan by her side as husband, and he had a heart operation as a child. But that's where the similarities end between them.

Born Frank Walters, Tristan hides his past under a new name. His relationship with his wife, Alannah, is fraught with anger. Alannah has seemed like a different person since the car accident, and lessons of the past have taught him not to trust too easily.

Will Tristan and Lana learn enough from past mistakes to give them a second chance at love?

Be transported to another world on a breath-taking ride into the unknown, where two lovers will come to find the true meaning of forever. Return to Me is a heart-wrenching tale of love, loss, and rediscovery that draws you in from the first page.

Buy *Return to Me* now and lose yourself in a world where second chances make anything possible.

About the Author

Mae Archer knew she wanted to be a writer since she was a child. She loved listening to her grandmother's war stories about English maidens falling in love with handsome Yankees while England burned under the Luftwaffe's blitz.

When she discovered romance novels as a teenager she soon realized that her dream job was to be a romance writer. After many career twists and turns she's making her dreams come true.

Mae's real life is like one of her grandmother's stories. She met a foreigner who traveled through Australia and it was love at first sight. She married him six months after they met and every day since has been an adventure. She lives in Australia with her husband and daughter.

Mae has been an avid reader of romance novels since she was a teenager and her own novels combine some of her favorite romance tropes including time travel, second chances and star-crossed lovers.

Mae Archer is the pen name for author Amra Pajalic. Amra writes young adult contemporary fiction under her own name and dark fiction as A.P. Pajalic.

SIGN UP FOR AMRA'S AUTHOR NEWSLETTER

For news, giveaways, bonus material, and sneak peeks, please sign up to her newsletter below.

www.amrapajalic.com
CONNECT WITH AMRA

g goodreads.com/author/show/3310015.Amra_Pajalic

f facebook.com/AmraPajalicAuthor/

instagram.com/amrapajalicauthor/

https://twitter.com/AmraPajalic

tiktok.com/@amrapajalic

youtube.com/c/AmraPajalicAuthor

PLEASE LEAVE A REVIEW

If you enjoyed this book and would like to show Amra your support, please consider leaving a star rating and/or review on the website from where you purchased the book.

Also By

Romance as Mae Archer
Return to Me
Hollywood Dreams
Vintage Dreams
That One Summer Anthology

Memoir
Things Nobody Knows But Me
Growing up Muslim in Australia

Young Adult
The Cuckoo's Song
Sabiha's Dilemma
Alma's Loyalty
Jesse's Triumph
The Climb

Dark Fiction/Horror as A.P. Pajalic
Woman on the Edge

www.ingramcontent.com/pod-product-compliance
Lightning Source LLC
Chambersburg PA
CBHW061535210726
48287CB00006B/1962